Dragon Mountain

Dragon Mountain

By Daniel Reid

TUTTLE PUBLISHING
Tokyo • Rutland, Vermont • Singapore

Disclaimer: This is a work of fiction. The names, characters, places and incidents contained herein are either the products of the author's imagination or used fictitiously. Any other resemblance to actual people or locations is entirely coincidental.

First published in 2005 by Tuttle Publishing, an imprint of Periplus Editions (HK) Ltd., with editorial offices at 364 Innovation Drive, North Clarendon, Vermont 05759.

Copyright © 2005 Daniel Reid

All rights reserved. No part of this publication may be reproduced or utilized in any form or by any means, electronic or mechanical, including photocopying, recording, or by any information storage and retrieval system, without prior written permission from the publisher.

Library of Congress Control Number: 2005926981
ISBN: 0-8048-3788-0

Distributed by

North America, Latin America & Europe
Tuttle Publishing
364 Innovation Drive
North Clarendon, VT 05759-9436
Tel: (802) 773-8930
Fax: (802) 773-6993
info@tuttlepublishing.com
www.tuttlepublishing.com

Asia Pacific
Berkeley Books Pte. Ltd.
130 Joo Seng Road
#06-01/03 Olivine Building
Singapore 368357
Tel: (65) 6280-1330
Fax: (65) 6280-6290
inquiries@periplus.com.sg
www.periplus.com

Japan
Tuttle Publishing
Yaekari Building, 3rd Floor
5-4-12 Ōsaki
Shinagawa-ku
Tokyo 141 0032
Tel: (03) 5437-0171
Fax: (03) 5437-0755
tuttle-sales@gol.com

First edition
09 08 07 06 05   10 9 8 7 6 5 4 3 2 1

Printed in Canada
Design by Linda Carey
TUTTLE PUBLISHING ® is a registered trademark of Tuttle Publishing.

**United States of America
Central Intelligence Agency
Bangkok**

To: Director/Covert, Langley, Virginia
Re: Operation Burma Road
Class: CONFIDENTIAL
Date: February 21, 1981

Captain Jack Robertson, who served as one of our main operatives in Southeast Asia prior to his disappearance on a mission in northern Laos on Sept. 2, 1971, reappeared at our Embassy office in Bangkok last week. We have commenced debriefing him, and a transcript of the information he has given us so far is attached herein for your reference.

Robertson was in charge of Operation Burma Road when he went missing. His mission was to organize a network of agents and informants in northern Burma and Laos to help us monitor the activities of Burmese Communist troops, the Shan Freedom Army, the Karen Liberation Front, and other insurgent groups operating throughout the region, where they all engage in opium trafficking and heroin production to finance their operations. Robertson's account of his nine-year captivity in a remote region of northern Burma is difficult to verify because his abduction knocked out most of our contacts in the Golden Triangle, and only he knew the key links. We are currently trying to reconfirm details of his deposition through independent fieldwork and will forward any new information to you as it becomes available.

I

I know this is all being transcribed for the record, but I'm no writer, so I'll just tell my story exactly as it happened, start to finish, without any fancy frills. Then I want a one-way ticket out of this place so I can go home and find my family.

My name's Jack Robertson, and I'm—I was—senior pilot for Air America, operating out of Saigon from 1962 until my last flight in September 1971. I hear that Air America folded up several years ago and that we let Saigon fall to the Reds. We're still holding the line in Korea and Taiwan, so what the hell happened to us in Vietnam?

Anyway, I remember the day it happened as clearly as if it were yesterday. It was September 2, 1971, and I'd just flown a load of ammo and communications gear from Saigon up to our forward supply depot in northern Laos, the one near Luang Prabang. It was a routine run, and I expected to be back in Saigon by nightfall.

As usual, there were a couple dozen people hanging around the airstrip, hoping to hitch a free ride back to Saigon. But we had so much opium stockpiled in the hangar for my return run—forty lugs, as I recall—that there wasn't enough space left on board for a fly to squat and shit, much less for extra passengers. Due to the short runways up there, we were still using DC-3s on that run, so we had to watch our weight carefully.

When the cargo bay was fully loaded, I grabbed the mailbag, climbed into the cockpit, and took off around 3:00 PM. I'd just reached cruising altitude when the shit hit the fan.

I'd heard some creaking back in the cabin, but assumed it was caused by all those heavy lugs of opium settling into place as I banked sharply toward the southeast. I had just lit a cigarette when a big wet wad of red betel juice sprayed past my face and splattered onto the instrument panel. I spun my head around and found the stubby barrel of an Israeli-made Uzi machine gun pointed at my face. My first thought was, "Where the hell'd he find a weapon like that in this part of the world?" It was a moot question.

Looking up at the man behind the trigger, I saw that I was in for some big trouble. Square and squat in the cabin door, betel juice dribbling like blood down his chin, there stood a filthy, bald-headed Chinese with one eye missing. A sweat-stained patch covered the empty socket. Yes, I'm sure he was Chinese—after thirty years out here, I can identify Asians at a glance.

So there stood this one-eyed Chinaman grinning at me like a maniac with red-stained teeth, casually aiming an Uzi at me. I knew that a three-second burst from that gun could inscribe the Lord's Prayer on my forehead, so I didn't pull any monkey business. I just froze and stared him down.

To my utter amazement, he addressed me politely in Chinese, using my old Chinese name. *"How are you, Mr. Luo?"* he sputtered in lousy Mandarin. His accent told me that he was a southern Chinese and that he felt uncomfortable speaking the northern dialect. *"The Boss has sent me to greet you and to accompany you back to his place for dinner. He is very eager to see you again."* Immensely amused by his little soliloquy, he burst out cackling, spraying stinking red spittle all over the cockpit. He obviously knew who I was and that I speak Chinese, so I decided not to fake it.

"This is a bit sudden," I replied in Mandarin that put his own

pronunciation to shame. "*Unfortunately, I have a previous engagement in Saigon this evening. Please thank your boss for his kind invitation. Perhaps some other time.*"

That really cracked him up, and his eyes slit shut with laughter. If he'd been holding anything else but that damn Uzi, I would have tried to overpower him right then and there, but a cockpit struggle with that piece would have been the end of both of us.

"*No way!*" he replied in a nasty tone. "*If I don't bring you back in time for dinner tomorrow evening, the Boss will tear out my other eye and make me eat it. Aye-yah, he has such a terrible temper!*"

So that's how the whole thing started. "One-Eye," as I called him, would not tell me who the "Boss" was, nor where we were headed for "dinner." Instead, he eased himself comfortably into the copilot's seat and handed me a neatly folded piece of paper with a curt message scrawled in English:

> Captain Jack, long time no see! I request the
> honor of your company for dinner at Dragon
> Mountain. My emissary Mr. Huang is an experienced
> navigator, and he will direct you here. If you refuse
> to cooperate, he will kill you.
>
> Best Regards,
> Your Old Friend

Tucked inside the note was a crude map with precise navigational directions inscribed on it. One-Eye jabbed a dirty finger at a point on the map and told me that it was our destination. I could see at a glance that the point was located on the Shan Plateau in northern Burma, on the western outskirts of the Golden Triangle.

With One-Eye riding shotgun and spraying betel juice the whole way, we cruised north across Laos, skirted along the Thai border, and entered Burmese airspace right smack over the Triangle. The radio squawked a few times, but whenever I reached for the receiver, One-Eye jabbed his Uzi in my ribs.

I checked my bearings and began to descend slowly near the

point indicated on the map. Steep mountains and dense carpets of green jungle stretched all the way to the horizon without a trace of civilization anywhere. Was I supposed to land in the trees?

But as we got closer to the ground, One-Eye blinked in recognition at the terrain below. Clucking his approval, he craned his neck against the window and scanned the landscape. Suddenly, he pointed toward a huge craggy mountain that loomed like a dark tower against the northern skyline.

"*There it is!*" he slobbered. "*Dragon Mountain!*"

We veered around the northern face of the mountain, and signs of human habitation began to appear below: squat thatch huts, green patches of land under cultivation, terraced rice paddies, dogs and water buffalo, smoke from cooking fires—all the elements of a typical Asian village. One-Eye directed me ten miles further north, where a tattered wind sock flapped listlessly, indicating a landing strip. The coolies below looked like busy ants as they scurried across the strip to clear away the camouflage.

"Okay, Huang, fasten your seatbelt; we're going in!"

"*Good, good!*" he sprayed, watching the tricky landing with his single, well-practiced eye. "*Your flying skills are excellent. The Boss will be very pleased!*"

II

As soon as we'd landed, the barefoot coolies swarmed across the airstrip again, dragging shrubs and fallen limbs to conceal it. I taxied to a halt under a makeshift canopy among the trees that served as a hangar and disembarked, with One-Eye right behind me, prodding me in the ribs with his Uzi. Dented drums of gas and oil, broken boxes full of rusty old tools, and sundry aircraft parts were strewn about the ground. Amid this mess an old woman squatted before a charcoal fire, stirring a bubbling cauldron of what appeared to be food. One-Eye commandeered a fresh chew of betel from her, then nudged me up a jungle trail with his gun.

The hike up to Dragon Mountain took a day and a half. We spent the night in a filthy hovel along the trail, which One-Eye called an "inn." It was actually a guardhouse, and I spent a sleepless night chained to a post like a dog.

We finally reached the village I'd seen from the air late the following afternoon. A crude drawbridge fashioned of wooden planks and bamboo beams hung across a muddy, swift-flowing stream that separated us from the final stretch of trail into the village. One-Eye barked a sharp command at the guards on the other side, and immediately they lowered the bridge to let us cross. We trudged along another half mile or so of trail into the village, a dusty little hamlet perched on a plateau at the foot of that massive mountain.

It looked like a typical Shan village, with thatched huts built up on short bamboo stilts, each one set in a private yard enclosed within hedges of tough thornbush. A few Shan tribesmen eyed me curiously as we passed through the village, but they didn't show the least hint of surprise at my presence there. They all wore the towel-like turbans, baggy pants, and loose tunics favored by the Shan, who resemble Mongols and Tibetans more than Burmans. Their Chinese-Tibetan ancestry gives them features entirely different from Southeast Asian stock.

I stopped to light a cigarette, but One-Eye poked me rudely in the ribs and hurried me on. "*No time to stop and rest now. Almost sunset. Boss waiting. Dinner soon.*" We passed through the village and headed up a steep path that led directly to the base of Dragon Mountain.

The dirt path gave way to smooth stone steps as we approached a huge, triple-arched Chinese gate, like the ones you see in old Chinese temples and imperial palaces. A fifteen-foot-high stone wall with cornices of glazed yellow tile snaked out into the jungle in both directions from this gaudy gate. For a moment it reminded me of a stage set for one of those corny Chinese kung-fu movies they make in Hong Kong. Nothing seemed real.

One-Eye shouted the same command he'd used at the drawbridge, and one of the side gates slowly swung open. Only the "Boss" used the big central portal, One-Eye informed me, just like the Chinese emperors of yore. Armed guards, all of them Chinese, milled around within the compound, but they too barely took notice of me.

Have you ever seen the private imperial gardens located in the northern compound of the Forbidden City in Peking? That's what the scene that unfolded before my eyes behind that gate looked like. Not a trace of the wild jungle through which we'd trekked to get there was to be seen anywhere within those walls. Instead, everything was neatly landscaped and carefully manicured, with exotic trees and flowers from all over the world growing profusely in well-tended gardens. There were "mountains" of cleverly sculpted rocks, "rivers" formed by little rills that connected carp ponds abloom with lotus, miniature stone bridges, ornate pavilions, and other classical Chinese touches. In the soft pink light of dusk, the scene looked especially beautiful—and unreal.

We followed a flagstone path through the gardens up to another huge Chinese gate. It too swung open at One-Eye's signal. We entered a spacious courtyard paved with slabs of raw marble, empty except for an enormous bronze incense cauldron, five times the size of an oil drum, set in the middle. A pair of intricately cast golden dragons snaked up the sides of the cauldron, peering ferociously at each other over the rim.

Long colonnades of rooms stretched along the walls on both sides of the courtyard, with the smooth gray face of the mountain rising abruptly opposite the gate. This cliff soared about a hundred feet straight up, with the craggy peaks of the mountain towering high above it. Halfway up the face of this cliff, I noticed windowsills jutting out. A heavy double door studded with bronze spikes formed an entrance to the cliff at ground level. Chiseled in bold relief just above the door, writhed an impressive Imperial Dragon, the kind with five claws rather than only four, the symbol of Chinese emperors for over five thousand years. Whatever lay behind that door must have been carved into solid rock.

"*We are here!*" One-Eye hissed with obvious relief, his mission accomplished. The bronze doors swung open silently, and he signaled me inside, while he remained out in the courtyard as the huge doors swung closed again behind me.

I found myself standing in a vast cavern, dimly lit by a few coconut oil lamps along the walls. It was so large that I couldn't see the ceiling. Suddenly a woman stepped out of the shadows and greeted me with a deep bow, her hands folded before her heart in the traditional Buddhist gesture of greeting. Though she was definitely of local stock, she wore a tight-fitting Chinese gown of the finest silk brocade. Silently she led me across the dark, dank cavern to a narrow stairwell carved into the living stone of the mountain and beckoned me to follow her up.

It was a long climb, and when we emerged at the top, I saw why. We now stood in a chamber set high above the cavern I'd entered down below. Plenty of light and fresh air entered this room through latticed windows cut into the stone walls, and Chinese lanterns with electric light hung from the carved wooden beams of the ceiling. The entire room was paneled in richly lacquered hardwood, and the scent of sandalwood incense sweetened the air. Traditional Chinese furnishings stood all around. It looked like one of those throne rooms in the Forbidden City, where Chinese emperors used to receive foreign dignitaries.

My escort melted into the woodwork as silently as she'd appeared, leaving me to gawk at the incredible luxury that filled the room. But the smell of tobacco told me I was not alone. Perched on some kind of elevated throne at the far end of the room sat a man smoking a cigarette and tapping the arm of his chair with the tip of a long gold, jewel-encrusted fingernail sheath that capped the little finger of his left hand. He glared at me in stony silence as I approached him.

At ten paces I froze in my tracks and squinted at the man. I could hardly believe my eyes! A smug smile spread across the man's face as he felt my recognition grow—a demented smirk that confirmed his identity beyond all doubt. Sure, he'd changed a bit—lost most of his hair and much of his bulk—but that look on his face—especially the perverse smile—hadn't changed at all. Swank on his pretentious throne, wearing a long Mandarin robe of the best Chinese silk, with a golden dragon embroidered across his chest, sat my "old friend" Ching Wei, grinning at me through a coiling cloud of smoke.

III

"*Have you eaten yet?*" he asked. That's a standard Chinese greeting and means basically the same as "How do you do?" in English. It was typical of that wise guy to greet me with such courtesy, as though he'd simply invited me over for dinner, rather than having me dragged there at gunpoint by his goon, One-Eye.

"*Not yet,*" I replied, which immediately obliged him to offer me something to eat. I hadn't had a bite of food for two days and felt famished.

"*Good!*" he said, snuffing out his cigarette in an ivory ashtray as he stood up. "*Dinner is ready. I am so delighted you could come here tonight. As our great sage Confucius said, 'When friends visit from afar, is this not indeed a pleasure!'*"

He led me through a round "moon door" into a smaller but equally well-appointed dining room. Scrolls of elegant Chinese calligraphy and delicate landscape paintings adorned the walls; sprays of fresh flowers artfully arranged in antique porcelain vases scented the air—all the traditional trappings of a classical Chinese gentleman were there. In the middle of the room stood a polished rosewood dining table, set for two.

"*Please be seated,*" he said, indicating my place at the table.

We sat silently and appraised each other for a few minutes. He had grown one of those long "Fu Manchu" types of mustaches, which he habitually twisted and tugged with his fingertips. The nail of his left little finger must have been at least two inches long, and it was sheathed inside a gold nail scabbard studded with emeralds, rubies, and sapphires that sparkled in the candlelight. This indicated, in classical Chinese fashion, that he was a gentleman of wealth and leisure, not a man of labor. His smoothly shaven head shined like a bowling ball, and his eyes flickered brightly through narrow lids. Another native girl in Chinese dress appeared from nowhere and poured us a round of hot rice wine—the real Hsiao-Shing wine from the mainland. She also placed a few platters of hot hors d'oeuvres on the table, served us a portion of each, then disappeared as silently as she'd come.

"Welcome to Dragon Mountain, Captain Jack," Ching Wei finally said, hoisting his cup to toast me. "Let us drink to old times. Bottoms up!" His English had improved considerably since I'd last seen him. "How long has it been, Jack?"

"About thirty years."

"Ah, yes, thirty years. We have so much to talk about, and so much time to talk about it. But first, we must eat!" He clapped his hands and the girl returned with the first course, a platter of roasted meat and braised poultry, garnished with coriander, scallions, and a savory sauce.

The girl returned about every fifteen minutes, each time with a fresh platter of the most superb Chinese food I'd eaten in years. One bite was enough to tell me that a genuine culinary artist was at work back in the kitchen. We had everything from bird's nest soup to shark fin stew, and some dishes that I'd never even tasted before. We didn't spoil the meal with serious discussion. Instead, we chatted about the finer points of Chinese cuisine.

By now this whole thing must sound like a fairy tale, so let me backtrack a bit and fill in the background.

I first met Ching Wei back in Chungking, China, during the war. We were both pilots then, assigned to fly supplies over the Himalayan Hump from India into Kunming and Chungking. I was stationed there from 1942 until VJ Day in 1945, when I was transferred back to Shanghai. So I knew Ching Wei for about three years there, after which I never saw him again until that night.

The first time we met was at a Chinese martial arts class that we both attended in Chungking. The weather was so terrible there that we'd often be grounded for days at a time with nothing to do. And with the chronic shortage of fuel, the constant damage to runways from Japanese bombs, and the endless bickering between General Stilwell and the Chinese command, we ended up spending more time on the ground than in the air. The martial arts class helped kill time.

There was a remarkable old Chinese master living in Chungking at the time, and he organized the class especially for Chinese and American officers stationed there. I guess the class was his personal contribution to the war effort. We simply called him "Old Lee" among ourselves, but always "Master Lee" to his face. He came from a long line of martial artists and Taoist mystics, and—believe it or not—his father was still alive then at the ripe old age of 273! To prove it, Old Lee once showed me his father's birth certificate, duly stamped with the official seals of the Kang-Hsi reign in the Ching Dynasty. I once asked his father for the secret to his health and longevity, and he simply replied, "Correct breathing." Anyway, it was fascinating stuff, and it had both recreational and practical health benefits. I always looked forward to the class during those long dismal days we were grounded.

About thirty of us studied under Old Lee—ten Americans and the rest Chinese—but at any given time about half of us were stuck on the other side of the Hump in India. It was like a little fraternity: close bonds of brotherhood formed among most of Old Lee's students. That's the Chinese way.

During my three years with him, I grew quite close to Old Lee. He seemed to like me from the start. Later, I realized that he saw something in me that aroused his professional interest as much as his personal friendship.

Old Lee said that I was unusually sensitive to the vital force that the Chinese call *chi*, the essential energy of life that animates all living things. With proper training and lots of practice, Old Lee said, I could learn to focus and direct my chi by virtue of will power, first by practicing martial arts forms, and later by meditation and other internal methods. Old Lee took a dim view of the war-whooping, high-flying, muscle-bound variety of martial arts. Instead, he cultivated the soft, subtle internal powers of chi. *"Properly applied,"* he often said, *"four ounces of energy can topple one thousand pounds."*

Old Lee also entrusted me with his highest teachings. He knew from long experience that most young adepts end up abusing the powers of the martial arts if taught its innermost secrets too early in life. But he felt that as a foreigner who had taken the trouble to learn the basics of Chinese language and culture, I had demonstrated sufficient sincerity to be taught these esoteric arts the way they were meant to be practiced. So I learned a lot from Old Lee, and in the process we became good friends as well.

Because he taught me so much in private outside of the regular class, some of his Chinese students grew very jealous, especially since I was a foreigner. It didn't seem fair to them that the old man would teach me—a "foreign devil"—precious Chinese secrets that he kept hidden from them, but Old Lee ignored their resentment and trusted his own instincts.

My privileged position with the master irritated Ching Wei more than it did anyone else, and before long he thoroughly disliked me. But in typical Chinese fashion, all this personal discord remained well hidden below the surface. Chinese society demands harmony among classmates and colleagues, even if it's only superficial. Moreover, my superior performance both in class as well as in the cockpit of a plane demanded at least his grudging respect. That's also the Chinese way.

Eventually, it became clear that Ching Wei was doing more than just flying military supplies over the Hump. Somehow, he amassed an enormous fortune in gold, and being young, arrogant, and Chinese, he flaunted it for all to see. He bought a huge villa on the outskirts of town, where only the top brass could afford to live, then filled it with luxuries available only at great cost on the black market and moved in a few fancy women. In those days most of us couldn't find a beer or a cigarette in Chungking for love or money, but Ching Wei had plenty of both and much more to boot. He lived like a Chinese general.

"*He is an arrogant and small-minded man,*" Old Lee used to say of him. "'*Dog bones wrapped in human skin.' Pay him no heed.*" But the rest of the guys really resented Ching Wei's blatant profiteering, even though corruption was so common throughout the Chinese command that there seemed little point in reporting him.

Old Lee and I made frequent excursions into the rugged mountains of western Szechuan, outside Chungking. We visited ancient temples and spent many a night in remote mountain monasteries with raggedy old monks who invariably turned out to be founts of wisdom. Several times we visited an old friend of his who had retired to a distant mountain cave to meditate in complete solitude. His name was Ling Yun, which means "soaring in the clouds." He'd been living in that cave for over five years when I met him. It was during these excursions into the mountains that Old Lee taught me his most important lessons, and I can't blame him for being so secretive about them. In China, the most profound teachings and techniques have always been transmitted orally from master to select disciple, precisely to prevent jerks like Ching Wei from gaining access to them.

My navigator, Sam Conway, and I were in charge of all pilots and crew flying the Hump in and out of China, and it didn't take us long to figure out how Ching Wei was making all his money. Actually, his own navigator exposed him after Ching Wei refused to give him a bigger cut of the action. The navigator was bright enough to know that if he reported Ching Wei to the Chinese command, he'd only get himself in trouble, if not killed, for rocking the boat. So he reported Ching Wei directly to me. That set the stage for what happened next.

His navigator reported that Ching Wei had been using his aircraft to smuggle opium from India to China. Since the Japanese onslaught had cut Chungking off from all domestic Chinese sources of opium, users there paid enormous prices to get the stuff. Back in those days, opium was as much a part of the Chinese diet as rice and tea—and often it was more plentiful than both. Almost everyone smoked the stuff. So, for the fat-cat addicts of Chungking, India became the only viable source, and Ching Wei, the only available supplier, of their precious opium. After the big shots finished smoking the good stuff, the pipe heads were scraped out and the dross was sold again to coolies and clerks who couldn't afford anything better.

Ching Wei's ploy was clever: he had his ground crew in India replace half the military and medical supplies bound for Chungking in his aircraft with opium. The food, medicine, and other supplies he left behind served as the payoff to the ground crew to keep their mouths shut. When he landed in Chungking, his own boys unloaded the crates, juggled the delivery ledgers to account for the missing supplies, and stashed the opium in a warehouse near town. He greased a lot of palms along the way, but since the entire scam depended solely on him and his plane, Ching Wei took the lion's share of profits. Had he not been so greedy, his navigator would never have blown the whistle on him.

This sort of thing was standard operating procedure in the Chinese military, so for a while we let the whole thing ride. But as his greed grew, Ching Wei dumped more and more supplies in India so that he could bring more and more opium into China, causing a critical shortage of food and medicine for the wounded who kept piling up in Chungking's hospitals. Pretty soon Ching Wei was getting as effective as the Japs at killing Allied troops. Sam and I no longer had any choice: we reported Ching Wei directly to the U.S. command.

Colonel Boyd went through the roof when he heard our story. He was ready to go find Ching Wei and shoot him on the spot, but so much bad feeling had already been generated between the Chinese and American commands in the wake of Stilwell's recall from China, that the bust had to be handled just right to be effective.

We found out from his navigator when Ching Wei's next opium run was scheduled, and that afternoon Colonel Boyd decided to inspect all incoming supplies personally. Inspections were, of course, routine, but they'd always been conducted by

Chinese officers who were paid to inspect things, as the Chinese put it, "with one eye open and one eye closed."

Ching Wei landed right on schedule and taxied to a halt at his usual spot on the tarmac. It was a cold, overcast day, with drizzling rain. Ching Wei's crew swarmed around the plane and began unloading the cargo bay just as Colonel Boyd and three armed aides came squealing around the corner in a jeep. They screeched to a halt right in front of his open cargo bay, while Sam and I watched the whole thing from a discreet distance.

You should have seen the look on Ching Wei's face when he stepped off the ladder to find the colonel and his aides prying open his crates with crowbars. He protested loud and long and made dire threats, but all to no avail. The colonel inspected every single crate, and when he'd completed his tally, he found a total of 1,800 pounds of raw opium stuffed into various boxes marked "Medical Supply" and "Food." He arrested Ching Wei, loaded the crates of opium onto a truck, and drove straight over to the Chinese command, with both the culprit and the evidence in hand.

To make a long story short, the Chinese finally court-martialed Ching Wei, but only after heavy pressure from General Chennault, who vowed to bring the matter to the personal attention of his good friend and patron Madame Chiang Kai-shek herself. No one in China ever wanted to get on the wrong side of that ruthless dragon lady, especially on the subject of opium, for not only did she personally detest the Chinese opium habit, she was also a devout, God-fearing Christian with a missionary zeal to stamp out what she referred to as "China's Shame." So Ching Wei was officially court-martialed rather than given the usual slap on the wrist, and to further mollify the U.S. command, they handed him a stiff ten-year sentence in the brig, but needless to say Ching Wei never served a day of it. As I recall, it cost him $10,000 per year to get his sentence reduced to zero, which means he had to cough up a $100,000 bribe—a hell of a bundle in those days.

A few weeks later, a mangled corpse was hauled into town on an oxcart. The peasant who brought it in complained that the body had "fallen from the sky" and landed in his pigsty, killing a pregnant sow. Since the body wore a Chinese uniform, the old farmer had brought it to the Chinese military base in town for disposal—and to demand compensation for his sow. The corpse belonged to Ching Wei's navigator.

Before hurling him to his death, Ching Wei must have forced the navigator to tell him how he'd reported the scam directly to me, because a few days later he confronted me on the street as I walked home from Old Lee's place. Neither my Chinese nor his English were very good back then, so it was almost a comical encounter.

"Why you telling Amelicans me selling opium?" he demanded, barely able to contain his rage. "Now no plane, no business, no face!"

"Forget about face, Ching Wei, yours isn't worth saving." If there's one thing I can't stand about the Chinese, it's their absurd attachment to "face." Here they were, losing their asses in the war, and all they worried about was gaining "face."

My remark made him so furious that he had to switch over to Chinese to express himself. *"Fuck your mother's stinking cunt!"* he shouted for openers, invoking the favorite Chinese curse. *"You know perfectly well that half the officers in Chungking play the black market! Why not report them all?"*

"The others buy and sell cigarettes, beer, soap, and other things, but they're not depriving dying men and orphans of the food and medicine they need to stay alive." I fished for a Chinese flourish and came up with *"Yours is the worst kind of drunk!"* I'd meant to say "crime," not "drunk," but the two words are pronounced exactly the same except for the intonation, and I blooped it.

He laughed at that, but not for long. *"I should kill you here and now!"* he threatened. Ching Wei, like most Chinese, would never face a dangerous adversary alone, so I knew he had a couple of armed goons standing by in the alley.

"Go ahead. If you kill me, the colonel will come after you again, and you know there's no place left to hide in China except Chungking, unless you want to take your chances with the Japs. And if the colonel doesn't get you first, Old Lee will. You know perfectly well that the master does not tolerate fighting among his students."

He'd been smirking, but when I mentioned Old Lee, his face grew dead serious. *"The master knows of this?"*

"He knows everything. In fact, he saw through you long before the rest of us did."

That clearly upset him. *"You filthy bastard of a barnyard sow! I will let you go this time, but remember these words: somewhere, some day, I will find you again, and then we will settle our accounts!"* With that parting shot, he spun around on his heels and disappeared down the alley, his henchmen muttering and shuffling behind him.

So that's how I met Ching Wei. When I left Chungking in 1945, I never thought I'd see him again. In fact, I'd completely forgotten about him until that evening at Dragon Mountain. I had no idea how he ended up in Burma, but I intended to find out.

"Did you enjoy the food?" he asked politely as we sipped fragrant jasmine tea. The last dish had just been cleared from the table.

"Excellent! That's the best Chinese food I've had in a long time." That was no lie. Despite my predicament, and with the help of all the good food and drink, I felt great. This would not be the last time I forgot my real situation in Ching Wei's presence.

"Good! Now let us take brandy and cigarettes in the parlor. We have business to discuss."

IV

"You must admit that you never thought you'd see me again. Correct?" Ching Wei swirled his brandy in a hand-cut crystal snifter, savoring the fumes like a cat sniffing the wind. We sat near the latticed windows on lacquered teakwood chairs cushioned with silk. A warm breeze blew the fragrance of night-blooming jasmine trees into the room.

"That's right," I admitted.

"But in recent years I have followed your career with great interest from—as we Chinese say—*'behind the curtain.'* Obviously, it is your fate to fall into my hands, for Heaven put you directly in my path." He cleared his throat and lit a fresh cigarette. "For your convenience, I will speak in English. I have an excellent English tutor here—a real Englishman—and my command of your language has improved considerably since our last conversation in Chungking.

"As you know, after America defeated Japan, Chiang Kai-shek and the entire Nationalist Chinese government moved their capital back to Nanking. Chungking looked like a ghost town after they left. I like the term 'ghost town'; the image is very Chinese. In any case, I moved back to the provincial capital of

Szechuan in Chengdu, where I planned to settle down and go into business.

"But when the Communists took Manchuria and wiped out the Nationalist army at Huai-Hai, all of us in the south knew that they would soon come to claim all of China. Our lines of communication and transportation with the last Nationalist strongholds in Nanking and Shanghai were completely cut off, so we could not join them in their final escape to Taiwan. By 1949, the only Nationalist generals still fighting our cause on the mainland were Lee and Duan, who held a small corner of free territory deep in the southwest. As the Communists advanced south, Lee and Duan made preparations to evacuate their men and materials to Burma. As a trained pilot, I was recruited to assist in the evacuation."

"Despite your court-martial?"

Ching Wei laughed. "Come now, Jack, by that time even convicted criminals were dragged from jail and put into uniform. In fact, I was fully reinstated as a captain. By the end of the year, Lee and Duan had established a secure base in the mountains of northern Burma. They were convinced that Chiang Kai-shek would soon launch a counterattack from Taiwan, so they committed their men and arms to daring raids across the border, harassing the Communists at their weakest points. We had eight thousand men when we arrived in Burma, and for years we continued to fight the Communists. In those days, we were still patriots. You may also be interested to hear that our old teacher, Master Lee, joined our march into Burma, and he remained here with us for eight years." That was the first mention of Old Lee I'd heard since the war.

"At first, the Nationalist government in Taiwan supported our campaigns against the Communists in China. For years we received regular deliveries of arms and other supplies from Taiwan. Most of this material was dropped to us by air."

"I know. One of my first assignments for Air America when I arrived in Taipei was to drop supplies into Burma for Lee and Duan. They were big heroes in Taiwan then." Prior to my transfer to Saigon in 1962, I was senior pilot in Taipei for nearly ten years, and I remember very well how popular the Chinese freedom fighters in Burma were in Taiwan in those days.

"How interesting that you were involved in those supply drops! You see, Jack, our fates are indeed entwined. But in 1958, all assistance from Taiwan was suddenly terminated, without explanation. By 1960, our troops in Burma looked like beggars—dressed in filthy rags, underweight from lack of food, no medicine for the wounded and sick." I resisted the urge to remind him that he had left our men in Chungking in precisely the same state by dumping food and medical supplies in India and substituting opium. "We all felt tired and homesick for our families and friends in Taiwan. Even Lee and Duan were refused permission to return. Why? They let us fight their cause for so many years here in Burma, then suddenly terminate all support and leave us to rot like dead dogs in the jungle. Never will I understand—nor forgive—this betrayal!"

"I don't understand it either, Ching Wei. When orders came down to halt our supply drops over Burma, it surprised the hell out of us too. No doubt it was some dirty political deal with China. Maybe Taipei made an agreement with the Reds to stop supplying you in Burma in exchange for a truce in the Taiwan Straits. They were shelling Matsu pretty heavily that year, as I recall. Anyway, we've never been able to crack Chinese intelligence in Peking or Taipei, so whatever's been going on between the two for the past twenty years remains a mystery to us. Chinese can't seem to keep a secret from each other for more than a few minutes, but they have no trouble keeping foreigners in the dark forever."

Ching Wei took that as a compliment and smiled. "Anyway, it does not matter anymore," he said. "What happened next is common knowledge. We had to survive. At first, we earned a small income by providing armed escorts to protect local opium caravans moving from the highlands of Burma down into Thailand and Laos. Although many of our senior officers found the opium business distasteful, it was—and still remains—the only viable source of income in this region, which you Americans call the 'Golden Triangle.' Our choice was quite simple: trade opium or starve to death.

"For several years we managed to survive in this manner without sacrificing discipline and unity. But greed and corruption follow the opium business like wolves follow the scent of blood. Junior and middle officers became addicted to opium smoking, and this soon gave them new ideas. First one, then another, then half a dozen different groups disappeared into the mountains and went into business on their own. Some extorted money from the villages that grow opium; others joined bandit gangs. Many died of disease and addiction, and even more were killed in bitter fighting among rival bands. I myself selected sixty good men from my outfit and established a small camp in the mountains. We had sufficient ammunition and supplies to last us about three months."

So far, Ching Wei wasn't letting me in on any big secrets with his postwar history—most of it was already common knowledge. What he was really doing was gloating about his own personal success. He certainly knew that I worked for the Company, and that Air America was only a front, but since he never intended for me to leave Dragon Mountain alive, he wasn't worried about telling me all the details of his criminal activities either.

"We settled near a village protected by a gang of local bandits. They were camped comfortably by a river in the valley, while we fortified ourselves high up in the mountains. They suspected neither our presence nor our intentions. One night, as their entire camp got drunk celebrating a local festival, we attacked them by surprise, killing more than half their men. The rest joined my forces. I now had a secure camp, a small but well-equipped army, and a prosperous village to supply all of our needs—my first kingdom!" He beamed with pride at the recollection.

"Of course, my operation was small in the beginning. We had to avoid contact with big, well-protected dealers at all cost. I moved my opium overland to Chiang Mai, in northern Thailand, using a long and difficult route through the mountains, where we would not be noticed. There I sold it directly to my own Chinese contacts, without meddlesome local middlemen.

"Then in 1965, I made my first—and only—mistake." The

memory clouded his face, causing his lips to twitch in silent rage. "I received an order for fifteen tons of raw opium, the biggest deal I'd ever made. Previously, I had never sold more than five tons in one transaction, but by then I had over two thousand men under arms and felt confident that I could handle it. My own villagers produced less than ten tons that year, so I raided neighboring villages to obtain the rest.

"I had never dealt with anyone but my own people before, but this time the buyer was General Rammakone, supreme commander of the Laotian Army—if you care to call those lazy, opium-smoking peasants an army. If I'm not mistaken, General Rammakone was also on your 'Company' payroll at that time, supposedly to fight the Communist Pathet Lao." He snorted with laughter at the irony. "The general's real business, however, was refining opium into heroin in an old Pepsi-Cola factory right outside of Vientiane! Much of it he sold directly to the Communists in North Vietnam, who turned around and fed it to American troops fighting in South Vietnam. Nasty business, isn't it?

"The deal was organized by my contacts in Chiang Mai. The general bargained hard for a lower price, but since he offered to pay entirely in gold bullion, we struck a bargain. It was a golden opportunity for all of us. We were instructed to deliver the opium to a remote camp in northern Laos. But I was dealing with strangers who were not Chinese, and therefore secrecy was impossible. The transaction soon came to the attention of Colonel Hsu, who at the time commanded the largest regular battalion of Nationalist troops remaining in the region. If Hsu permitted fifteen tons of opium to leave Burma without taking a share, not only would his dominant position in the trade be threatened, he would also lose face before his own troops."

"Heaven forbid that anyone should lose face!" I couldn't resist that remark, but he ignored it.

"You can imagine what happened next. Though I took a very difficult route, Colonel Hsu knew exactly when our caravan left camp and exactly where we were going. The moment we crossed the Mekong River into Laos, he attacked us in full force." Ching Wei trembled as he recalled the event, and his voice curled into a snarl. "They ambushed us from two sides as we crossed the river. They killed two hundred fifty of my men. They shot our pack horses in midstream, and much of the opium was washed downriver.

"We might have all been killed that day if General Rammakone himself had not intervened. When his scouts reported what was happening, the general took immediate action—not to save us, but to save his opium. He called in fighters and helicopter gunships and attacked both sides with rockets, napalm, and cluster bombs. Our men panicked, and both Hsu and I retreated back across the border into Burma. Meanwhile, the general's troops swept onto the battlefield and combed the river to collect the remaining opium. The general kept his gold as well. But that was not the end of the matter.

"As soon as we had crossed back into Burma, Hsu regrouped his forces and attacked us again, killing or capturing half my remaining troops. I returned to camp with less than five hundred men, convinced my days were over. I also carried back a souvenir from the battle to remind me forever of that black day—a piece of shrapnel that still remains buried in my liver." That explained his habit of favoring his left side whenever he sat down: any pressure on his right side caused the shrapnel in his liver to shift position, a sensation as painful as a knife in the gut.

"After that battle, Hsu thought I was finished, perhaps even dead, and that his monopoly on opium trafficking in the region was secure. But, as you can see for yourself," he swept an arm around his lavish throne room, "I am neither finished nor dead. I thrive!"

"Congratulations."

"Thank you. But my recovery was not easy. It required three years to reorganize my forces. First I raided small caravans and villages like a common bandit, avoiding all serious conflicts until I had rebuilt an even bigger army of three thousand men." He pounded the arm of his chair. "Then I came here and took Dragon Mountain away from Colonel Hsu! He had grown soft and fat, and his men had lost all discipline. We found his sentries sound asleep as we penetrated his camp one morning at dawn, and by noon this mountain was mine! Hsu and some of his men escaped north into the Kachen Hills, where he still conducts a petty opium operation. One day I will hunt him down and kill him off like the crazy dog he is!"

"Now that you're king of the mountain, why not just go in and kill him now?"

"Although I control over eighty percent of the opium trade here, it suits me to permit a few small dealers to continue their operations in the region. It confuses the authorities."

"Clever. You take all the profits, and they take all the blame." His smug narrative was starting to grate on my nerves.

"I see you tire of my talk, so I will come directly to the point," he replied sharply. "I learned two basic lessons from that disaster in 1965. First, deal only with Chinese buyers. Among Chinese, certain understandings and civilized principles always prevail when doing business, even among enemies. A Chinese buyer, for example, would have let Hsu and me fight to the finish, then deal properly with the winner, rather than try to kill us both and steal the entire shipment.

"The second lesson I learned is that moving such bulky and precious cargo overland, especially in this terrain, is an open invitation to trouble. Caravans are highly vulnerable to attack, even by small gangs of bandits. But hiring armies to escort and protect large caravans is so costly that it drives the price of opium beyond reason, which is not good for business. So I have taken inspiration from the old days, when we flew the Hump between India and China. From now on, I will move my opium by air!"

"Smart move."

"Yes, very. And that, Captain Jack, is precisely why you are here. You will be my pilot!" He threw his head back and cackled at the irony of my position, but his pleasure was cut short by a sharp stab of pain from the shrapnel in his liver. "What you had me court-martialed for in Chungking thirty years ago, you will now do for me here," he hissed through clenched teeth, finally revealing the audacity of his scheme.

"I have followed your movements very carefully since you moved to Saigon from Taipei to take over Air America operations there. However, military security at airports in Saigon, Bangkok, and other cities along your routes prevented me from taking action earlier. So I waited and I watched. When you started making those runs to northern Laos to pick up opium for your Company, you suddenly became available to me. You see, Jack, all this time your Company has been buying its opium from me!"

Ching Wei smirked at my surprise. Though we'd been buying and selling opium out here for years to finance covert operations that Congress refused to acknowledge, we'd always assumed the stuff came directly from the Shan, Karen, Hmong, and other mountain tribes that grow it as a cash crop. We had no idea we were dealing with the kingpin himself. As it turned out, all of our orders were channeled through Ching Wei's agents, who had it delivered anonymously to our pickup point near Luang Prabang. We never inspected the cargo, never kept ledgers, and never asked any questions. And to make sure that word of this did not leak to the outside, only I and two other senior pilots flew those opium runs, with no copilots as witnesses. It had been a simple ploy for Ching Wei to stash a goon with a gun in one of the opium lugs to nab me. I'd been a sitting duck.

"Ironic, isn't it?" he gloated. "Thirty years ago, you had me arrested and court-martialed for smuggling opium into China. Today you have been trapped at the same game, smuggling opium to Saigon for your CIA. And from now on, your duty will be to smuggle opium for me!"

"I had you busted because your little opium business deprived dying men of food and medicine!" I shouted, beginning to lose my cool. "I'm not in this for the money—to me it's just another cargo, like ammo or bananas or people. It's just part of my job."

"Fool! The problem with your CIA is that they wrongly assume that whatever they do is right. You know as well as I do that they engage in the opium trade to finance illegal political activities in Southeast Asia, activities so distasteful that even your own government refuses to acknowledge them. As usual, you Americans hide behind your flag and plead patriotism whenever someone accuses you of wrongdoing in the world. In fact, however, you are no better than us—and much less honest!" He paused to calm his voice, twisting the tips of his mustache. "Besides," he crooned, "you lie when you deny personal profit as a motive. What about the three hundred eighty thousand dollars you have accumulated over the years in the Hong Kong and Shanghai Bank in Hong Kong? Does the CIA really pay such handsome salaries?"

I was astounded that he knew so much about my private affairs. I felt stark naked. "All right, all right, so I turned a little profit on the side. Everyone out here does it. It's one of the fringe benefits of putting up with all this shit. A man's got to think about his retirement." But he'd caught me off guard, and my argument sounded weak. At least he did not seem to be aware of the network of fledgling agents I'd been secretly organizing in the Triangle through our contacts in the opium business. His interest in me was purely personal, not professional.

"Forget it, Ching Wei! I'm not flying dope around for you or any other tinhorn warlord. Thanks for the dinner and drinks, but no thanks!" I rose to leave, but had no place to go.

"Sit down and have another brandy, Jack. It may be a long time before you taste brandy again. Here at Dragon Mountain, one must prove himself worthy of such luxuries." I sat down, lit another cigarette, and accepted another brandy.

"That's better. Now listen carefully. It will be at least one more month before my next shipment of opium is collected, prepared, and properly packed for transport. That will give you time to adjust to your new life here." He spoke as if I were a new kid on my first day at summer camp. "You are not my only foreign guest here. Others enjoy my hospitality as well, and you will meet them soon enough.

"Like everyone else, you shall live as an honored guest in the home of a good family in one of my villages. The family will feed you and care for all your needs, and the head of the household will be held responsible for your welfare as well as your behavior. Believe me, he and his family will watch you night and day. Because if any of my guests tries to escape, his host and his entire family are killed, one by one, in the village square." He paused to let that sink in while he drained his brandy.

"On the other hand," he added, "guests who voluntarily decide to settle down here enjoy many benefits. Foreign guests remain in the homes of their assigned hosts only until they choose to marry local women and start families of their own. That is the Chinese way. You may select any girl from any village within my domain. When you marry and have children, you may build your own house in or near the village responsible for you. I will provide all materials and furnishings. In addition, permanent settlers receive monthly rations of foreign luxuries from the shop I keep in the main village. Razor blades, soap, whiskey, magazines—everything is available there. If you wish, you will also receive free opium, the very best. Guests who refuse to marry and settle down remain permanent burdens to their hosts."

Before I could say another word, he clapped his hands impatiently, and the girl who'd shown me in appeared from the shadows. "She will take you out to the gate. Huang is waiting outside to take you back to the village and introduce you to the family I have selected for you. In one month I will summon you again. At that time, I will give you good reason to work for me without the slightest hesitation or thought of escape."

He pointed at the stairs. "Now go!"

V

Ching Wei was right. It was good that I had another brandy while I had the chance. For the next six weeks I ate nothing but rice and barley with fiery curries that burned twice—once going down, and once again coming out. The natives were all devout Buddhists or hopeless opium addicts, or both, so they didn't touch booze. Some of Ching Wei's white hostages distilled their own *arack* from millet or palm, but that stuff burned even worse than the curries.

There seemed to be lots of white men around, but I rarely saw more than two or three together in the same place. Each went about his own business as if he were walking down Main Street, USA. Some had gone native, with local wives and children, and lived in their own native huts. Others remained perpetual guests of their hapless hosts and flatly refused to conform to local customs. To the great disgust of the natives, most of the unmarried white men stayed stone drunk much of the time, occasionally abusing their hosts as well as each other in drunken brawls. But the villagers had strict standing orders from Ching Wei to make his "guests" feel at home there, so no one dared protest the behavior of these drunken louts. The first phrase I learned in the local lingo was, *"Liquor is as natural to the white man as milk is to babies."*

One of Ching Wei's whims, to which he devoted increasing attention over the years, was to collect a sort of menagerie of white captives to amuse him. This hobby he pursued with great enthusiasm. When I arrived, he had about fifty men in his collection; by now there are at least three hundred fifty. Each captive lives in the household of his assigned host and receives everything he needs without having to do a lick of work for it. Those with special skills—like me—lived in the main village near the mountain, where Ching Wei could beckon us at will. But basically we were free to do anything we pleased—except leave.

One of our main functions was simply to amuse Ching Wei, like a collection of exotic pets. Whenever the mood struck him, he would invite a bunch of us up to his place for a huge feast and lavish entertainment. The more drunk and disorderly his guests became, the more he seemed to enjoy their company. He himself rarely drank more than a glass or two of champagne or cognac, but it was clear from his glazed eyes and manic grin that he had something a lot stronger than booze coursing through his veins.

White men were not his only whim. He also collected exotic animals from all over the world—mostly predators—and these he kept in a zoo within the palace walls. The animals were tended by an English veterinarian specifically selected and kidnapped for that purpose. When he felt particularly perverse, he'd sometimes pit one of his pet predators, such as a tiger, against a guest or native who'd broken one of his rules.

Ching Wei also collected guns and orchids. I saw his gun room several times over the years, and I doubt there's a single type of firearm produced in the last hundred years of which he doesn't own at least one sample. That's where One-Eye got the Uzi he used to nab me.

Ching Wei's orchid collection contained over five hundred varieties. He kept an elaborate, fully automated greenhouse tended by a French orchid cultivator named Moreau, whom he also kidnapped expressly for the job. Ching Wei once explained to me the source of his endless fascination with orchids. He said the blossoms reminded him of the intricate, delicately convoluted folds of the female genitalia, each breed displaying its own unique shape, size, and colors, each blossom exuding its own individual fragrance. "Everything about the orchid is designed to arouse sexual excitement in the roving butterfly or passing bee," he'd often say while sniffing lovingly at a bloom. When you think about it, he's right.

Except for the foreign luxuries brought in from Bangkok, Dragon Mountain was entirely self-sufficient. The Shan tribesmen grew food in great abundance, with staples of rice, millet, and barley, and all sorts of fruits and vegetables for variety. For meat, Shan hunters stalked their prey throughout the surrounding mountains and valleys with vintage carbines, bringing back monkey, small deer, wild boar, water rats, civet cats, and snakes. The only domestic animals they ate were dogs and pigs, and those only on special occasions. The natives observed a strict taboo against eating beef, for the cow and buffalo were sacred animals to them, but because their white guests preferred beef above all other food, the locals were forced to butcher cattle for them. I soon learned another native term for the white man, always muttered in a tone of deep disgust: "*The Beefeaters.*"

Security was no problem at Dragon Mountain. Ching Wei deliberately kept his domain as inaccessible as possible. The massive mountain dominated the entire region, and the village at its foot was heavily fortified. This village served as the administrative center for his entire domain and was called Poong. His palace sat high above the village, most of it carved directly into the living rock on the mountain's northern face. The palace was surrounded by five acres of elaborate gardens, and the grounds were completely enclosed within a tall corniced wall. The only access to the palace from the village was the steep path I'd taken with One-Eye the first night.

The terrain was ribboned with swift, torrential rivers and carpeted with jungles so thick that light rarely reached the ground. The only way into Poong from the outside world was the drawbridge I'd crossed with One-Eye the day I arrived there. To get to other villages from Poong, you first had to cross the bridge, then take one of the narrow trails that branched off into the jungle on the other side of the river. The trails were all guarded around the clock by armed sentries and trained hunting dogs. Ching Wei kept the trails so narrow and overgrown that no wheeled vehicles—not even a wheelbarrow—could negotiate them. Booby traps were planted everywhere, and only the guards knew their locations. Careless natives wandering about without permission occasionally got killed or horribly maimed by these traps.

Uninvited intruders were spotted and killed long before they even got near Poong. As for captives bent on escape, even if they miraculously managed to get by the watchful eyes of hosts, guards, and dogs, they still faced a gauntlet of uncut jungle crawling with predators, snakes, poisonous insects, and bandits. And if that didn't stop them, then the Wild Wa headhunters who infested the region did. No one had ever escaped from Dragon Mountain and lived to tell about it.

When I left the palace that night, One-Eye was waiting outside to escort me back down to the village, where he brought me to the house of my assigned host. The size of the hut and garden indicated a family of relative wealth and prestige. This was no doubt Ching Wei's idea of honoring an "old friend."

Except for a single oil lamp sputtering through an open doorway at the top of a rickety bamboo staircase, the entire house lay wrapped in darkness. An old man snoozed on a bamboo stool just inside the threshold, his back propped up against the mud and wattle wall. He wore the turban, tunic, and loose pants favored by the Shan, which, incidentally, means "the free people." One-Eye climbed the steps and woke the old man with a swift kick in the ribs, muttered something at him, then disappeared back into the darkness.

The old man blinked at me with glaucous eyes as he stood up to greet me. He stretched and yawned, then motioned me to follow him inside the house. We crossed the main room, where I noticed a few bodies stretched out asleep on reed mats. The whole place reeked of curry, garlic, and charcoal. Groping his way through a narrow hallway, which gave access to the back of the house, he led me into the room farthest in back. This was no doubt a precaution aimed at protecting his family from the white man's notorious smell, that rank, musty odor that the Chinese describe as "fox-stink."

Inside the room he lit another lamp, swept his hand around, then pointed at me and said something. I shrugged. He shrugged back. Suddenly we both burst out laughing—the unwilling guest meets the unwilling host—and I knew instinctively that we'd get along fine.

He pointed to a cot of jute webbing stretched over a wooden frame, the kind we used to call a *charpoy* in India. Next to it stood a crude table with a clay washbasin, a large jug of water for washing, and a smaller jug for drinking water. He lifted the lid of an old wooden chest: inside lay two moth-eaten blankets, a pair of baggy Shan pants, a wraparound sarong for wearing around the house, a bamboo cup, and a wooden bowl.

"Thank you," I said.

"San-kew?" he repeated quizzically, pointing at me. "Kiang!" he trumpeted, cocking a thumb at himself by way of introduction....

"Glad to meet you, Kiang. My name is Jack—not San-kew."

"Jacknut San-kew!" he said, nodding with approval.

"No, just Jack. Jack, Jack, Jack."

He tested the word a few times under his breath, then flashed a broad betel-stained smile to confirm it. "Jack!"

"Kiang," I pointed to him. "Jack," I cocked a thumb at myself. We grinned and nodded at each other, then he tucked both hands against the side of his head and made a snoring sound to indicate that it was time to sleep. I bobbed my head in agreement, and he backed out the door, bowing and grinning the whole way. Shucking boots and pants, I stretched out on the cot, smoked my last cigarette, and fell sound asleep.

I awoke next morning to find three young girls hanging in the doorway staring at me. I winked at them as I rolled out of bed, and they went flying like startled birds.

The first thing I noticed was my own sour stench. It was hot and humid there, and I hadn't been out of my underwear for almost three days. I've lived in Asia long enough to know that "fox-stink" is the one thing about white people that offends Asians above all else, so I stripped naked and squatted down by the wash basin to scrub myself as clean as possible with my handkerchief and water. Then I wrapped the sarong around my waist, stepped into the straw sandals by the cot, and headed down the hallway.

The main room was full of smoke from a cooking fire, which smoldered in the far corner. An old woman squatted by the coals, stirring some sort of porridge. The girls stood against a wall gazing at me, all three of them wearing faded sarongs and short sleeveless blouses that left their bellies exposed. The old woman wore the black, nondescript gown that all Shan women adopt after the age of forty. When I entered the room, she turned her head and grunted a command at the girls. Immediately one of them led me to a bamboo stool at a low table, while another brought me hot tea, and the third set a bowl of steaming hot porridge before me. There were several saucers of condiments on the table to spice up the porridge, which turned out to be a blend of barley, millet, and rice. It wasn't bad—if you don't mind garlic, chili, onions, and fermented fish paste with your morning cereal.

Kiang appeared just as the girls were serving me a second portion of porridge. He sat down next to me and applauded my appetite, as if I were doing him a great honor by eating his food. His eyes reflected not the slightest hint of resentment at my presence there. Perhaps the sarong and sandals, plus my timely morning bath, made me seem a bit more civilized. I later noticed that most of the white men there clung stubbornly to button-up shirts, tight trousers, leather shoes, and other items of Western clothing, despite the extreme discomfort that such clothing causes in that sort of climate. And they bathed so rarely that even I felt offended by their odor. Most of the white men there also spurned the native food as no better than cow dung, insisting instead on eating beef and bread. As for me, after so many years of living in Asia, I felt very comfortable with both the local diet and the way of dressing, and I had no trouble adjusting to either.

Kiang puffed on a crinkled black cheroot that looked like a dried turd. He offered me one, and one of the girls fetched a glowing twig from the fire to light it. As we sat there contentedly puffing cheroots and sipping tea, Kiang commanded his three daughters to come and stand before me. They giggled and lined up obediently.

Kiang then rattled off a rambling speech in the local lingo, aiming his bony fingers at me and the girls as he spoke. They appeared to be between fourteen and eighteen years old, though it's hard to tell with Asians, especially women.

I indicated that I had not understood a word he'd said by shrugging my shoulders and muttering in Chinese, *"I don't understand."* Though I did not expect him to understand Chinese, it somehow seemed more appropriate than English.

Kiang's eyes lit up the moment he heard my words. *"You speak Chinese!"* he yelped with delight, clapping his hands. He said he'd picked up a bit of the language from dealing with Chinese overlords for so long. He spoke it with a very heavy Yunnan accent, no doubt the influence of Ching Wei's troops, and his vocabulary was limited to three or four dozen words, but in Chinese that's enough, and soon we were communicating quite well.

Pointing at his daughters, he asked, *"Which girl most pretty?"*

"All very pretty!" I replied. *"All three same."*

He looked scandalized and shook his head vigorously. *"One girl pretty,"* he insisted, holding up a single finger, *"only one."*

That confused me. Apparently he wanted me to compliment his most attractive daughter, so I looked them over again. They were all quite lovely, but the oldest one was running a bit fat in the gut, and the youngest hadn't quite developed the curves of a full-fledged beauty queen, so I chose the one in the middle. She was an absolute knockout, with big, dark doe eyes and long silky lashes, thick jet-black hair hanging in a single braid down her back, and a beautiful face with a flawless complexion. Her full firm breasts strained at her buttons, and the curves of her hips bulged through her sarong like an hourglass.

"*That one most pretty,*" I said decisively, pointing at her. The girl immediately clapped her hands against her mouth and dissolved into fits of giggling, while her two sisters shrieked and nodded knowingly at her. Then the three of them disappeared in a huddle through the door. Kiang looked very pleased.

Just then his wife stood up from the fire with a grunt, shuffled over to the table, and set a three-tiered lunchbox of woven bamboo before her husband. She was an enormous bow-legged woman, with a kind but work-worn face. Kiang placed his palms together and bowed in the traditional Buddhist gesture that means "hello," "goodbye," and "bless you" all in one, then he grabbed his lunch and headed out to work in the fields.

I finished my tea alone and wandered into the village. Most of the men had already gone off to the fields to farm, or up to the hills to hunt and fish, while the women busied themselves hauling water from wells, washing clothes by the river, winnowing grain, and screeching at their children. No one paid me much notice.

A smooth dirt path bisected the village, which ran about a hundred fifty yards from end to end. Compact huts of mud and wattle with thatched roofs and shaded verandas stood on short stilts on both sides of the main path. In each yard grew at least a dozen areca palms, source of their beloved betel nut. In the middle of the village the path widened to form a sort of public square or plaza, shaded by several enormous pipal trees. The pipal, which looks like a banyan tree without the branch roots, is called the *bodhi* tree by the natives. Buddhists regard the bodhi tree as sacred because the Buddha attained enlightenment while meditating beneath the shade of a bodhi tree 2,500 years ago in India. Every bodhi tree in the village had a small shrine erected against its massive trunk, with fresh offerings of fruit, sweets, flowers, and incense always present.

I sat down on a rickety bench in the shade of the biggest bodhi tree in the village and looked around. I would have given anything for a cigarette. In the middle of the village square stood a big communal hut about sixty feet long, set on thick, squat stilts, but without any walls. It was an open pavilion that served as a sort of community center. Near it was a stone house of Western design, with corrugated tin roofing and real glass windows. Boxes and barrels of supplies were piled carelessly behind it. This turned out to be the foreign provisions shop to which Ching Wei had referred. Attached to the shop was a bar, where only Ching Wei's troops and white guests were permitted to drink. The bar suddenly reminded me of the outside world, and I wondered how my disappearance was affecting my family and friends back home. I cursed Ching Wei out loud.

"You must be new here," a voice rumbled over my shoulder. I leaped up and spun around to see who it was. There stood a tall, stooped, skinny white man dressed in sarong and sandals like myself. "My name is Moreau," he said, extending a limp hand. "I am the orchid man."

I introduced myself, and he sat down next to me. "The orchid man?"

"Yes, it is my duty here to care for Ching Wei's orchid collection. He has over five hundred varieties, you know, and almost three thousand specimens. Some are very rare. It is a big job." His voice was flat and listless, but there was no mistaking his accent: it was French. There was also no mistaking his condition: he was stewed to the gills on opium, his pupils shrunk down to the size of pinholes. He reached into his shirt for a pack of cigarettes and offered me one.

"Thanks, I just ran out of smokes last night. Where'd you find these?"

"These and other foreign goods are available at the shop over there," he replied, jutting his chin in that direction. "I live with my wife and child in a house over on the hillside just beyond the village." He pointed toward a densely wooded hill that faced Dragon Mountain from the far side of the village. "You must come to our house for dinner one night and tell me news of the outside world. I have been here already five years now." He gazed blankly across the village, his head bobbing rhythmically.

After a long silence, he stood up and stretched his limbs. "Well, I must go to work now," he said, and handed me the pack of cigarettes. "Please accept these; I have more at home. Where do you stay in the village?" I told him I was Kiang's guest, and he looked impressed. "Kiang is a good man. You are lucky. He has a big house and three beautiful daughters. You should be quite happy there. I will see you again soon, monsieur. Au revoir."

I sat there in a funk for the rest of the day, smoking Moreau's cigarettes and daydreaming. What else could I do? Soon the sun was sinking over the trees, and men began trickling back to the village from the hills and fields. Smoke from cooking fires curled up through thatched roofs, giving the impression that the whole village was aflame. The smell of fresh food and spices cooking reminded me how hungry I felt, so I left my roost under the bodhi tree and strolled back to Kiang's house.

He was already home and puffing on a cheroot when I returned, and he welcomed me with a cup of hot tea. Soon his wife and daughters had dinner ready, and we all gathered around the table to eat.

Except for festival days—when they slaughtered a pig or dog—dinners there were usually the same. We each got a heaping bowlful of boiled rice, millet, or barley. In the middle of the table were three iron pots, each with a different curry in it. Two were always some combination of vegetables, while the third was usually chicken, fish, wild game, or eggs, depending on what was available that day.

They used no chopsticks or any other eating utensils. Instead, each person ladled some curry onto his rice, then used the thumb and first two fingers of the right hand to mash the grain and curry into little bite-size balls, which were then popped into the mouth. The left hand is never used for eating, because its function is to take care of business at the other end of the line, using water instead of toilet paper. The Shan always wash their hands and mouths thoroughly both before and after eating—an excellent habit.

After dinner, Kiang and I chatted for a while over cheroots, but I was in no mood for socializing that evening. Despite the unfailing kindness of Kiang's family, I felt like an alien who'd landed on an unknown planet. No one protested when I stood up early to say good night, bowing my head with hands folded at the heart, in the traditional manner.

I got undressed and lay down on the cot, using my sarong for a sheet. I thought of reading myself to sleep, but there was nothing to read, so I just stared at the bouncing shadows cast against the walls by the flickering oil lamp.

I was dozing on the edge of sleep, eyes closed and mind adrift, when I heard someone swish quietly into my room. Startled, I bolted up in bed and focused my eyes on the intruder. Standing there next to me with a broad ivory smile, naked to the waist, was the daughter I'd selected that morning as the winner of Kiang's little beauty contest.

Surprised and embarrassed, I moved to cover my thighs with my sarong, but she snatched it from my hands and flung it aside. Then she yanked a knot on her hip and her own sarong fell in a heap around her feet. Purring softly, she twined her arms around my neck and pressed her body gently down on top of mine.

VI

It was an old tribal custom, and I must say that it really made me feel at home there. Moreau later told me that it was a traditional form of hospitality practiced since ancient times by the Shan mountain tribes, though not by the Burmans down on the plains. If a tribesman had as his houseguest a man of superior social rank to his own, it was customary for the host to provide his esteemed guest not only with the best food and drink at his disposal, but also to offer him one of his wives or daughters to sleep with at night. This was regarded as a great honor to the host's entire lineage. But if a woman of the household were caught sleeping with a man of inferior status to her own family, she would be driven out of the house and banished from the village, if not killed by her brothers on the spot. Since Ching Wei bestowed superior social status on all of his so-called "foreign guests," this happy custom applied naturally to me.

Besides that, any family who provided a wife to one of Ching Wei's guests and thereby helped induce him to settle down stood to gain considerable fringe benefits, such as access to goods from the store and free opium.

Her name was Suraya, and she was only seventeen. No need to dwell on the details of our first night together, except to say that she came to me so sweetly, so full of warmth and feeling, and with such an open heart, that it felt as though we'd been lovers forever. She showed no sense of shame or sacrifice about sex and approached me with unabashed curiosity. As the Chinese would say, she was "ripe as a melon, ready to split." When we appeared at breakfast together late next morning, no one even raised an eyebrow.

I bumped into Moreau later that day sitting under the same bodhi tree, smoking and reading a rumpled newspaper. He congratulated me on my good fortune with Suraya, informing me that she was one of the most desirable girls in Poong. I bummed a smoke and asked him why he was not at work.

"Sunday is my holiday. My wife sent me down here to have some rice ground to flour." He jutted his chin at a dilapidated shack just off the village square. "The old man there does it for me on his grinding stone—three kilos of flour for one packet of cigarettes. Not bad." He smiled for the first time, showing teeth that looked like rusty nails.

"Where the hell'd you get that newspaper, Moreau? Got a subscription?" He was reading the French paper *Le Monde*.

"Oh, this also comes from the shop. They bring it sometimes from Bangkok with other foreign publications," he shrugged, "and sometimes not. It is two months old already, but here all news is fresh."

"So tell me, Moreau, how'd you end up here?"

"Like you, I was invited." He'd been a teacher at a small primary school for the French community in Bangkok, but his real interest and lifelong hobby had always been orchids. "That is why I moved to Thailand. There I could spend all my holidays and spare time up-country, studying and collecting rare orchids. There are species growing in Thailand that are found nowhere else on earth. It was a good life."

Then one year, he won several major prizes at an international orchid show held in Bangkok, and his name and picture got plastered all over the press. Ching Wei, himself an avid orchid collector, had attended the exhibit during one of his clandestine business trips to Bangkok, and he'd been deeply impressed by Moreau's work. So impressed, in fact, that the moment he got back to Dragon Mountain, he dispatched a team of goons to stake out Moreau's place for an abduction. He was easy to nab: no family, no servants, no pets—just him and his orchids.

"Without damaging a single specimen," he recalled laconically, "they brought me and my entire collection back to this place. For more than one year I lived in the village as an unwilling prisoner, and I refused to cooperate with Ching Wei. But time and boredom—as well as opium—dissolved my resistance, and soon I came to miss my orchids even more than my freedom. So I went to him and agreed to serve as his orchid man. By then he had a substantial collection, including my own, but it required much work. I married the daughter of my host, and Ching Wei built that house up on the hill for us. Now I have no wish to return to the outside world. I'm quite happy here in my own little world with my family and my flowers."

An old man hobbled across the square with Moreau's sack of rice flour slung over his shoulder. Moreau thanked him with a pack of cigarettes and transferred the load to his own shoulder with a grunt. "Come," he said. "If you are not engaged elsewhere, you shall be my guest for lunch this afternoon. We always eat well on Sundays. Perhaps you can tell me more recent news of the world than this old newspaper."

Moreau's house sat tucked in the shade of tropical fruit trees halfway up a hill on the northern outskirts of Poong. It was built entirely of timber and tile, not mud and wattle like the dwellings in the village. Orchids hung everywhere, many of them in full bloom, and the whole place smelled like perfume. A long veranda overlooked the garden, with a view of the village below, and in the distance Dragon Mountain hulked against the skyline. I could barely discern the curved eaves and green tiles of Ching Wei's palace through the foliage.

"Please make yourself at home," Moreau said, leading me to a chair of woven jute on the veranda. "I'll just tell my wife we have a guest for lunch."

He returned with two clay mugs brimming with a frothy white liquid. "Rice beer," he explained. "The arack the others make is too strong for my stomach, and I cannot afford the foreign liquors from the shop. But this is very good, easy to ferment at home, and no stronger than European beer. We make it once a week. À votre santé!" We clicked mugs and drank. It tasted a bit like yogurt or buttermilk and was slightly carbonated like beer.

While waiting for lunch, I filled Moreau in on the latest events in Saigon, Bangkok, and other places I'd been to recently. I think he wanted to hear the news more for entertainment than information, for he never once registered any intellectual interest in anything I reported, nor did he ask any questions. He seemed to view the outside world as an ongoing soap opera. He liked to keep up with the plot and fates of all the major characters, but if he missed a few episodes, or saw a repeat, he didn't mind.

Meanwhile, his wife set lunch out on a rattan table on the other end of the veranda and called us over to eat. Moreau introduced her as Loma, and she greeted me with the traditional Buddhist bow. She had the distinctive Tibetan-Chinese features of pure Shan stock, without a trace of the Malay ancestry that prevails in the lowlands of Burma. She stood two heads shorter than Moreau, and had a strong, well-fleshed body. Her face was perfectly round and quite pretty, and she wore her hair in a single thick braid that hung down to the bottom of her back. They had a three-year-old daughter, whom I caught peeking at me through the window slats.

Lunch was excellent. Moreau's stomach could not handle curries, so his wife had prepared half a dozen different dishes of assorted vegetables and meats, some of them served hot and others cold, some lightly cooked and others marinated raw in marvelous dressings. All ingredients were finely shredded or chopped to make the food easier to digest. Instead of rice, she'd prepared a stack of very thin rice flour pancakes, like French crepes, which we used to wrap the various dishes into a kind of "Burmese burrito." We drank plenty of rice beer, and for dessert she served a big platter of fresh tropical fruits in bite-size pieces, all peeled and impaled on bamboo skewers, with a bowl of thick fresh coconut cream as a dip. After lunch, Moreau and I returned to our chairs on the veranda and smoked cigarettes while Loma cleared the table.

As the afternoon wore on and our stomachs settled, Moreau began to fidget, and his mind kept drifting from the conversation. Finally, he stood up and suggested we go inside for an "afternoon smoke."

"Thanks, but this one's still going," I said, hoisting my cigarette.

"Mais non, I mean a *real* smoke!" He flashed one of his rare smiles and beckoned me into a small room adjacent to the veranda. There was a polished hardwood platform elevated about one foot off the floor, and the walls were devoid of decor, except for a niche housing a small Buddhist shrine. Following his example, I kicked off my sandals at the door and sat down on the smooth planks. Latticed screens diffused the afternoon light that filtered in through the window slats, and a faint breeze carried the refreshing fragrance of frangipani into the room.

"Lie down here," Moreau instructed with a suddenly authoritative air. "No, on your side—facing the lamp, with your head on that pillow." The "pillow" was a rectangular block of wood about a foot long and six inches thick, with a smooth depression on one side where countless other heads had rested. The "lamp" was a small jar of coconut oil with a cotton wick stuffed through its cork stopper and a smudged glass chimney over it.

Moreau fiddled for a while with some utensils arrayed on a lacquered tray of paraphernalia that lay on a mat between us. Then he lit the lamp, carefully trimmed the wick, set the chimney in place over the flame, and lay his head down on a wooden block facing me.

"You have never smoked opium?" he asked with a tone of mild surprise. He reached for a bamboo tube resting on a rack beside him and lovingly stroked its smooth, well-seasoned surface. It was an old Chinese opium pipe, the likes of which I'd often seen in antique shops in Shanghai right after the war. It consisted of a thick bamboo stem with an ornately cast silver saddle, an ivory mouthpiece on one end and a matching ivory plug on the other. Inserted firmly into the socket of the saddle was a clay bowl about the size and shape of a doorknob, with a small hole drilled into an aperture in the middle of its convex surface.

As he worked in the lamplight, Moreau transformed before my eyes. No longer the listless hunch I'd seen in the village, his face now glowed with enthusiasm, and his eyes sparkled with life. His hands fingered the pipe and accessories like a musician tuning his instruments.

"Now we are ready to begin," he sighed. He dipped the tip of a long, steel spindle into a tiny cup of thick, black syrup, then dangled the droplet over the chimney. It bubbled and spluttered, swelling and expanding like burning rubber. He dipped the gob into the liquid again and repeated the process several times, until it formed a sticky ball the size of a pea. With the tip of the spindle he kneaded the hot wad of opium on the smooth surface of the bowl until it gradually achieved the consistency of gum and its color turned slowly from dull black to chestnut brown and finally to a beautiful burnished gold. Then he rolled the golden pellet into a perfect cone, spun the cone swiftly in the hot spot over the lamp until it became soft as taffy, and inserted the cone quickly into the tiny hole in the bowl. Twisting the spindle a few times to release the cone from the shaft, he pulled the spindle out clean, leaving the wad of opium stuck around the hole like a little doughnut.

With the look of a man about the enter the gates of heaven, Moreau tilted the pipe over the lamp so that the wad of opium hung directly in the "sweet spot" over the chimney and started puffing mightily with a deep, rhythmic draw. As the wad of opium began to sizzle and vaporize, the sound reminded me of the gurgle made by sucking the last drops of a soft drink up through a straw. He kept puffing until the little wad shriveled up and disappeared completely into the hole, plumes of blue smoke trailing from his nostrils. It smelled strong and sweet, like licorice or burnt chocolate.

Then it was my turn. It took me a couple of tries before I got the hang of it, but finally I drew the pipe properly and got some smoke down my lungs. It tasted good and was not at all harsh on the throat. The key to smoking is to create just the right pressure in the tube and maintain a steady draw. The Chinese call it "Swallowing Clouds, Spewing Fog."

At first I felt nothing. "What's this stuff supposed to do?" I wondered aloud. After a while, I realized that I really did feel "nothing." I felt completely oblivious to all physical sensations such as heat and cold, hard and soft, and totally detached from the whole world. I couldn't even tell if I was standing up or lying down, and the hard wooden block under my head now felt as soft as a silk cushion. I was floating in a cloud of cotton candy and felt more deeply and profoundly relaxed than I'd ever felt before.

We puffed a few more bowls and talked for a while. But it was not like a normal conversation. What I said was not always a logical reply to what he'd said, and sometimes I simply tuned out and drifted off while he was still talking. But it didn't matter. We simply narrated whatever was passing through our minds at the moment, and some of it was pretty damn strange. At one point, I imagined myself to be a bird gliding silently on a warm summer breeze, and I proceeded to describe in great detail what it felt like to fly. Vivid fantasies popped in and out of my head in a random parade of images. I lost all concept of time and space and felt glad to be rid of them.

We must have laid there smoking and mumbling at each other for hours—it could have been days for all I knew. I kept shifting between normal awareness and a dreamlike state that lay somewhere between light sleep and gentle intoxication. The only earthly things that concerned me were the lamp, the pipe, and Moreau, who now seemed like the oldest of friends.

When Moreau finally helped me to my feet, it was already dark outside. My gut felt a bit jittery, but a few breaths of fresh air out on the veranda fixed that. I thanked him for the lunch and the wonderful smoke and wandered back down to the village in a pleasant and totally carefree reverie.

Suraya was awake and waiting up in bed for me when I got back to Kiang's house, but I found myself unable to rise to her charms. So instead, she gently massaged me to sleep.

VII

Six weeks later Ching Wei sent One-Eye down to fetch me. By that time I felt quite at home in Poong. Kiang treated me as part of the family, and Suraya was such a delight that I worried less and less about my predicament. I was still in bed with her when One-Eye called, and I appeared at the door in my sarong and sandals.

"*You must wear human clothing to see the Boss!*" he barked at me in Chinese, eyeing my native habit with undisguised distaste. He tossed a plastic bag at me. Folded neatly inside, I found a long Chinese robe of pure blue silk, similar to the ones Ching Wei wore, but without the dragon insignia. From now on I was to wear this outfit whenever visiting the "Boss," One-Eye informed me. I went inside to change, kissed Suraya goodbye, and followed One-Eye up to the palace.

"*What's up?*" I asked him as we hiked through the village. "*Another party?*"

Like most Chinese, One-Eye became a fountain of information when addressed in his own language. The inscrutable face that most Chinese present to foreigners masks nothing more than language and cultural barriers. The moment you bridge that gap, the mask melts away.

"No party," he replied, hawking betel juice along the path. "Now is time for work. Opium ready. Six thousand kilos. Start delivery today. You and I. This afternoon. After work finished, Boss make big party." One-Eye was not exactly eloquent in Mandarin, but he managed to make himself understood.

We entered the palace grounds through the main gate, but instead of heading straight up to the palace, One-Eye led me down a garden path that wound through tropical arbors to an open Chinese pavilion set on the banks of a carp pond abloom with lotuses. Inside sat Ching Wei, listening in rapture to a pair of rare songbirds trilling in a bamboo cage, while he tossed bread crumbs to the fish below. Beside him sat a gorgeous Chinese girl dressed in a sky-blue tunic and jet-black pants of polished Thai silk.

"Good morning, Captain Jack," he greeted me in English. "Please have a seat. I trust you have been enjoying your stay in Poong?" I nodded. "Meet my third wife, Mei-ling." She bobbed her head and stood up to pour me a cup of chrysanthemum tea, then excused herself with a curtsy and disappeared into the garden.

"Your wife is very beautiful," I remarked.

"Yes, I am very fond of her. I found her at a dance hall last year in Taipei. She is twenty. I bought her contract from the management there and also paid her family a small fortune for her, but she is worth the price."

He winked and switched over to Chinese. *"She is a natural-born white tiger, as smooth and fragrant as my most prized orchids."* In case you're wondering what a "white tiger" is, that's what the Chinese call a woman whose pudendum is totally and naturally devoid of pubic hair. All of Ching Wei's women were white tigers—that was another one of his eccentric Chinese whims—and this fetish was also reflected in his fascination with orchids. *"The heart of a woman's flower,"* he noted, *"looks exactly like that of an orchid, but can you imagine an orchid all covered with coarse hair?"* No doubt this whim at least partly explains why he kept no white women in his harem. I've run across a few white tigers over the years in Asia, but to me they always looked a bit strange, like a bald-headed woman. I guess there's just no accounting for a man's taste in sex.

"Taipei?" The word had given me a jolt. My son Duncan lived in Taipei.

"Yes, Taipei. I visit there from time to time during my business trips abroad, but only for the purpose of pleasure. Of course, I must assume a different identity there," he sneered sarcastically, "for we freedom fighters are not welcome in Taiwan. Even my wives do not recognize me when I leave Dragon Mountain." He poured some more tea and came quickly to the point. "Now, we have some business to discuss."

"I'm listening."

"Despite some minor problems in several villages, the first portion of this year's opium harvest is now ready for delivery. We have prepared and packed six thousand kilos." Every year at harvest time, Ching Wei conscripted men, women, and children from all the villages within his domain to gather the raw opium, a tedious process that requires each swollen bulb to be repeatedly scored by hand, then scraped of the precious sap that bleeds from the incisions. Since the opium and grain harvests often coincided, villages that were short of able-bodied labor sometimes fell behind schedule as they tried to salvage their food crops from ruin. But any such delays were always paid for in blood, so they were few and far between.

"You will fly this shipment of opium to northern Thailand, beginning this afternoon. It will require three flights, one per day, and One-Eye will accompany you all the way." One-Eye, who'd been idly standing by feeding the carp, perked up like a lapdog when he heard his name mentioned.

"What's to stop me from flying straight back to Saigon with your opium?" I figured it was time to lay a few cards on the table and see what he was holding against me. "Or maybe One-Eye and I could swing a little deal of our own. You don't really expect him to commit suicide by shooting me in midair if I try to escape?"

"If you attempt to escape, he will most certainly shoot you, but he will not commit suicide, not even for me. That is a stupid Japanese custom, not Chinese, as you well know." That smug smirk crept across his face again. "You see, Jack, Mr. Huang is also quite capable of operating the aircraft. He flew with me during the war. But, since losing his eye in that battle with Colonel Hsu in 1965, his vision has not been suitable for flying. He damaged my last aircraft beyond repair while trying to land it at a remote jungle airstrip, but he is nonetheless still capable of flying. And I assure you that he still sees clearly enough through his good eye to shoot you dead with that gun. It would be very difficult to miss with an Uzi."

"Sounds like you've got it all figured out."

"Yes, I do. But One-Eye is not the only one who will be watching you. My rivals would like nothing better than to shoot down my plane with a full cargo of opium on board. I am the only one in the region capable of delivery by air, and they would like to negate my advantage. Within five miles of Dragon Mountain you are safe at any altitude, but beyond that range I suggest you remain above five thousand feet, otherwise you will certainly draw ground fire. But, please, do not cruise above seven thousand feet—we do not wish to appear on radar screens in Bangkok or Saigon. Huang will keep his eye on your altimeter."

"Anything else?"

"Yes. Insurance, of course."

"Insurance?"

"In order to dissuade you from even dreaming of escape—by land or by air—I have arranged an insurance policy to protect my investment in you." Danger signals twitched inside my gut.

"Let me tell you more about my visit to Taipei last year." I felt a hollow spot grow in my belly as he spoke. "As I said, I visit Taipei only for pleasure, especially for Chinese food and Chinese women. One evening, my friends took me for amusement to a bar much frequented by American soldiers and foreign businessmen. It was called the Golden Lily Club." I knew the place well and had drunk there several times with my son Duncan. "As we sat there drinking, a young foreigner burst in through the door singing a Chinese love song! He was quite drunk, but his Chinese was absolutely perfect. The moment he entered the bar, he began to flirt loudly with all the girls, quoting erotic Chinese poetry from the Sung Dynasty. I was truly impressed by his command of Chinese and greatly amused by his behavior." Now I could feel the clincher coming.

"Soon a girl from another club charged in behind him and beat him over the head with her purse. To my complete amazement, he spun around on his stool and hit her back! The fight that followed provided the best entertainment of my entire visit to Taipei. They made a complete mess of the place, breaking glasses and turning over tables as they rolled around on the floor like a couple of wild animals. When the manager tried to stop the fight, he got himself kicked in the balls and bit on the wrist in the process." Ching Wei laughed long and hard at the recollection. "You know what I heard the manager say, Jack? He shouted, *'It's that drunken foreigner Luo Bao-shan again, destroying my bar and ruining my business!'* Imagine my surprise, Jack: Luo Bao-shan is *your* Chinese name!"

I felt too weak too respond, for I knew what this meant. It meant he had me by the balls, literally, in classical Chinese fashion: one mistake on my part and my son would end up a bloody pulp in the gutters of Taipei.

"So, of course, I asked my friends to find out about him," Ching Wei calmly continued. "A handsome, intelligent boy, though he drinks too much. This is what I discovered." He tossed a file at me. Inside were listed my son's name—Duncan Peter Robertson—his address, his job, and a brief rundown on his daily (and nightly) routines. There were several photos of him in front of his house, obviously taken with a telephoto lens. All the information was correct. I myself had given him the money to rent that house, and I'd personally arranged his job at a travel agency in Taipei owned by my old buddy Horatio Wu. "So you see, the boy in Taipei is my insurance policy against your escape."

I felt trapped and helpless. If I'd had a weapon on me, I think I would have wasted him right there and then, One-Eye and his Uzi notwithstanding.

"You're a coward and a dirty bastard, Ching Wei!" was all I could muster in response, but it rang hollow. Knowing he had me nailed, he just laughed it off, but his mirth was cut short by a sudden sharp stab from the shrapnel floating in his liver. His face froze in agony, and his mood turned black.

"In case your own son's life is not sufficient insurance against your escape," he snarled, "permit me to tell you what will happen to Kiang and his family if you try to leave here. His three daughters will be given to my bodyguards as slaves, a fate far worse than death. You will meet my bodyguards soon enough. Their cruelty surpasses the worst nightmare, and their loyalty to me is absolute. The old man will be skinned alive in the village square, and his wife slowly boiled to death in the cauldron in my courtyard. As they die, their corpses will be fed to my dogs." He was in too much pain to utter another word, so he signaled One-Eye to take me away.

VIII

We marched from the palace straight down to the airstrip, arriving there after dark. Next morning, I found the plane fueled and packed to capacity with neatly bundled lugs of opium. I made a routine inspection of the aircraft to make sure that everything was in place and noticed that the radio had been removed from the cockpit. The musty, bittersweet smell of raw opium was overwhelming.

We made three consecutive runs in three days, spending the nights in hammocks in the hangar. Our delivery point was a clearing in the jungle with a small landing strip somewhere in the northeast corner of Thailand. One-Eye navigated entirely by sight, so I don't know the exact bearings of the place, but I could find it again if necessary.

After landing, One-Eye would hop out and lock me in the cockpit. I couldn't even go back to use the toilet—had to piss out the window instead. But I could hear coolies grunting and cussing in Thai as they unloaded the opium from the hold and reloaded the cargo bay with crates of fancy food, liquor, cigarettes, magazines, and other provisions for Ching Wei's palace and the shop in Poong. These items were brought up from Bangkok and stockpiled in a warehouse near the strip for our return runs to Dragon Mountain.

With the season's first load of opium safely delivered and his palace replenished with luxuries, Ching Wei decided to celebrate by throwing one of his lavish parties. He did this after the successful conclusion of every major deal. "Ching," incidentally, is a common Chinese surname that means "celebration." "Wei," his given name, means "great." And that's how Ching Wei viewed life on earth: as a "Great Celebration."

These parties gave me the opportunity to meet other members of his menagerie. With the exception of Moreau, myself, and a few others whom Ching Wei wished to keep close at hand, most of his so-called "foreign guests" were quartered in remote mountain villages scattered throughout the far-flung corners of his domain, and they rarely appeared in Poong except by invitation or to purchase monthly provisions at the shop.

On the appointed day, we all gathered in the courtyard of the palace around mid-afternoon. Everyone wore a long Chinese gown like the one I'd been issued. Cushioned chairs were set around the big bronze cauldron that stood in the middle of the courtyard, and beautiful young Shan and Karen girls dressed in traditional Chinese style circulated among the guests with trays of drinks and snacks. I grabbed a Scotch from a passing tray and surveyed the scene. I counted over thirty guests, about half of them white and the rest Chinese, with a sprinkling of local village chiefs, called *sawbwas*. A sawbwa functions both as chief and shaman in traditional Shan society, and the position is hereditary. These fellows were colorful, highly eccentric characters who liked nothing better than a big party, and Ching Wei took great pleasure in cultivating their friendship.

Suddenly Ching Wei burst into the courtyard, closely trailed by six of his personal bodyguards. He called these thugs his "Black Dragons," and each one of them had a writhing black dragon tattooed across his bare chest. With heads shaved smooth as apples and bodies rippling with muscles, they were clearly bred for fighting and killing. None stood less than six feet tall—unusual among Chinese—and each wore baggy black pants tied at the waist with a green silk sash. Tucked into his sash, each carried a 9mm Browning automatic and a long curved blade.

"Them's his bloody Black Dragons," an Englishman named Todd Wellington whispered in my ear. Todd was an engineer by profession and had been at Dragon Mountain about five years. Like Moreau, he'd decided to "settle down" there, and his job was to design, install, and maintain all the various drawbridges, booby traps, and communications systems, and do other high-tech engineering jobs for Ching Wei. He'd also invented an ingenious sewage disposal system for the palace and for the village of Poong, which was a real blessing for those of us who lived there. He worked with local farmers on irrigation projects and did whatever else required the skills of a qualified engineer.

"Where the hell'd he find them?" I asked Todd. "It's not every day you see Chinese built like that."

"He buys or steals them when they're still young boys, then has the older guards train them to be mean as devils. That big one there," he cocked an eyebrow discreetly at a massively muscled guard who swaggered across the courtyard right behind Ching Wei. "That's Lai, Ching Wei's chief bodyguard: you don't want to even look the wrong way at that bastard. His favorite game is to see how fast he can spill a man's guts intact onto the ground with that blade he carries, without puncturing any of the vital organs, and I've seen him do it often enough. Ching Wei uses them Black Dragons to enforce the law around here and to protect his private quarters. I doubt there's a living soul in this whole bloody kingdom who hasn't witnessed them sods cutting up some poor bloke in public, or skinning him alive, or poking out an eye just for laughs." A shudder ran up his spine and jerked his neck. "Everyone here fears and loathes them, and they bloody well know it, which makes them even meaner. They guard their master like watchdogs twenty-four hours a day, and you'd have to kill all twelve of them before you ever got close enough to Ching Wei to do him any sort of harm. He treats them like prize pedigreed pets." Todd grabbed another Scotch and suggested we join the others, who were already seating themselves around the cauldron. "We don't want to hold up his bloody show now, do we?"

Ching Wei sat on a plush throne with his guests arrayed around him. He clapped his hands, and in through the gate a dozen performers came bounding—acrobats, jugglers, martial artists, dancers—all highly skilled and dressed in colorful costumes. The show lasted nearly an hour and was as good as any I'd seen in Hong Kong or Taipei.

As we applauded the final act, Todd leaned over and whispered, "Here comes the grand finale. Now you'll see for yourself why everyone's so bloody afraid of them Black Dragons."

Two of the guards hopped effortlessly onto the rim of the huge bronze cauldron, which stood about five feet off the ground and was over three feet in diameter. It was filled to the brim with the finely powdered ash produced by burning incense. Two more guards dragged a struggling man in through the gate and shackled his ankles to the big bronze feet at the base of the cauldron. Then the guards up on the rim reached down and grabbed the man's arms, stretching his torso as tight as a drum as they yanked him upward. Except for a flimsy loincloth, the poor bastard was stark naked, and his body glistened with the cold sweat of fear.

Ching Wei stood up and everyone fell silent. "Last time I demonstrated for your pleasure the Death of a Thousand Cuts, but, unfortunately, the man died after less than six hundred incisions. It seems that technique is a bit too delicate for my Dragons. So today, they will perform for you an even more ancient method known as One Man/Two Halves." He turned to his victim and introduced him in a voice ringing with disdain. "This man is a Communist spy from the Kachen Hills. He was caught gathering intelligence near a village on the edge of the Shan Plateau. The sin of Communism is unforgivable, and the only just punishment for a Communist spy is death." With that announcement, he nodded at his guards and sat down.

Todd leaned over again and whispered in my ear. "He calls his own bloody bandits the Shan Freedom Army, and all the others Communists. He hates Communists more than anything else on earth, and he always saves the worst punishments for them. For God's sake, don't make any remarks during this, and don't try to leave. I once saw a bloke get violently ill during one of these demonstrations, and when he stood up to excuse himself from the courtyard, Ching Wei told his guards to grab him and put him to death together with the original victim. Bloody awful it was, him screaming and pissing and puking all over the place." Todd drowned the memory with a long slug of Scotch.

A brawny guard was warming up with what appeared to be a long samurai sword. He swung the gleaming blade round and round, etching loops and figure eights in the air, the whistle of cold steel clearly audible. The terrified victim stood stretched like a frog ready for dissection, his eyes riveted on the blade which the guard now held aloft as he stood poised before him.

The whole thing took less than two seconds. The executioner stood at an angle that exposed the victim's torso fully to our view, then cocked his sword as far back as he could reach. With a single stroke so swift and sure that the blade could be heard but not seen, he severed the man in half just below the navel. His lower trunk crumpled lifelessly to the ground, while the guards on the rim of the cauldron jerked his torso up by the arms and planted it firmly in the bed of ashes before a single drop of blood spilled. Blinking with surprise, the man tested his arms for life, then grimaced and began to howl as the pain and realization sunk in.

"He'll be up there at least a day," Todd said, "alive as you and me. That ash is fine as talcum powder and will staunch the flow of blood to a very slow trickle. Poor bloody bastard!"

By then it was close to dusk, and Ching Wei rose to announce dinner. "Come, my friends, it is time now to eat and drink. The banquet table is ready!" We all stood up with relief and followed him inside. The half-man in the cauldron bellowed horribly, but the big, heavy doors of the palace swung shut and cut off his screams behind us.

There followed a fabulous feast of the finest Chinese cuisine anyone could hope for. There was a roast suckling pig—all cut up into bite-size pieces, then reassembled to look like the whole pig—snake and shark fin soup, braised deer livers, monkey paw stew, and two dozen other dishes. Hot Chinese rice wine accompanied the meal, and everyone rushed to get loaded in order to forget the grisly spectacle we'd witnessed outside.

Ching Wei barely touched his food, and he drank only enough liquor to participate in formal toasts. He kept getting up and milling around the table, toasting each guest in turn, explaining the finer points of the menu, telling jokes. I'd never seen him so cheerful. To him the banquet was just another part of the show, and we were the performers. The drunker we got, the happier he looked. For his guests, the banquet was an opportunity for an elaborate debauch. I've never seen men stuff food and drink down their gullets with such gusto and blatant self-indulgence as the guests at Ching Wei's table.

The banquet lasted three or four hours, and all the while, scantily clad native girls pranced around the table, performing some kind of erotic folk dance. After the meal, we were served French cognac, English cigarettes, and Chinese tea. Everyone burped and grunted with satisfaction, and no one left the table sober—least of all me. Although I was introduced to all the guests at the party that night, the next day I felt so hungover that I remembered only Todd, who'd counseled me wisely throughout the evening.

I also remembered all too clearly the rude awakening we got as we filed out of the palace later that night. In our drunken revelry, we'd conveniently forgotten about the man slowly bleeding to death in the cauldron, but there was only one exit, and it led right past him.

A full moon glowed in the sky, illuminating the entire courtyard in a pale silver luminescence. As we passed the cauldron, the man's terrible gurgling and garbled appeals for help served to remind us of the fate that lay in store for anyone who offended Ching Wei. After all those hours of feasting and laughter, the sound and sight of the dying man—not to mention his stench—had a most unsettling effect on us, exactly as Ching Wei intended. The moment I got beyond the main gate, I chucked up the entire meal along the trail.

I stumbled back to my room at Kiang's and found Suraya still awake, waiting up for me as she always did. She looked so sexy and full of life that I was throbbing like a piston by the time I got my clothes off. But when I tugged at her sarong and tried to make love with her, she pushed me away and held me at arm's length.

"No, no," she bleated in the broken English I'd taught her. "No can do!"

"Yes, yes," I replied, thinking she was only playing coy. I grabbed my shaft and pointed at its swollen condition. "Yes, tonight, now!" But I was too tipsy and could not hold her down long enough to strip off her sarong and pin her to the bed. Tired and disgusted by her attitude, I finally gave up the chase, scolded her severely, and dropped into bed. With eyes cast to the ground like a chastened child, she slipped silently out of the room, and I fell asleep.

Much later that night, when the whole house was dark and quiet, she came back and crawled into bed beside me, waking me with a shower of kisses and urgent sighs. She pumped me up again, and we made love until we were both exhausted and fell asleep.

Imagine my surprise when I awoke next morning to find not Suraya, but her younger sister Chandra asleep in the crook of my arm! Suraya had been menstruating the night before, and Shan custom imposes strict taboos against sex or any other physical contact between men and women during that time of month. Seeing how horny I was, and dismayed by my anger, she had left the room and recruited her younger sister to come in and service me instead.

As it turned it out, that too was the custom there.

IX

A month later, the second shipment of opium was ready, and like the first, I delivered it in three consecutive runs to the same jungle clearing in northern Thailand. The Thai end of Ching Wei's operation was well protected by the northern Thai command, and we never had any trouble getting in or out of there. Bangkok turned a blind eye on Ching Wei's opium operation because he hunted down and killed more Communist insurgents than the Thai Rangers did. Like the Burmese government, Thai authorities regarded Ching Wei and other Chinese Nationalist warlords in the region as a convenient buffer between the Thai heartland and marauding Communist bands along the northern borders, and they were right. As far as Ching Wei was concerned, the only good Red is a dead Red, and he always reserved his most painful punishments for them.

For example, to celebrate the successful completion of the season's second delivery, he threw another party and demonstrated an ancient Chinese punishment known as the "Red Butterfly" on a pair of Bur-Coms caught snooping around the outskirts of his domain. The two men were stripped naked, then slowly impaled on thick, steel stakes serrated with sharp barbs, which gradually pried open and tore apart their loins like butterflied prawns. "This is an excellent method for extracting information from these Communist dogs," he said, lips quivering with pleasure at the spectacle. "But there is nothing they can tell me that I do not already know." The victims were screeching for mercy and spewing out all sorts of random information, but the Black Dragons continued to push their bodies down onto the stakes until their torsos split open and their guts slithered onto the ground like a bundle of writhing snakes.

Later on that evening, I met someone who we all thought was dead and gone. It had been seven years since I'd last seen him in Bangkok, and at first I didn't recognize him. But Ching Wei's introduction left no doubt who he was.

"Jack, I want you to meet an old friend of mine. I believe he used to work for the same company as you. This is Jim Thompson. Jim, meet my friend Jack Robertson."

"Well, I'll be dipped in shit! Jim! We all thought you were history by now!" Since Jim's sudden disappearance in Malaysia in 1967, we hadn't turned up a single clue in the case. His abrupt departure left a big hole in our Bangkok office—and a big question mark hanging over our entire Southeast Asian operation. Though I'd worked with him a few times on Company business over the years, and attended a few dinner parties at his house, we'd never been very close.

"Good! Glad to hear that everyone thinks I'm dead!" he laughed. "But as you can see, I'm very much alive and well." His hair had gone completely white, and he'd lost quite a bit of weight, but otherwise he looked fit, cheerful, and completely at ease.

There'd been all kinds of crazy rumors floating around about Jim before he disappeared. Some said he kept a harem of Asian women at his house and shared them with his friends. True, said others, but Jim himself was a confirmed pederast and had a particular preference for young Thai boys. Drugs, gambling, pornography, you name it—there was no end to the gossip about Jim Thompson.

He ran a highly successful silk export business in Bangkok, and with the money he made at that he built himself a luxurious

Thai villa and filled it to the rafters with expensive Chinese antiques. His dinner parties became legendary throughout Asia. He kept a small army of Thai servants—attractive young men and women dressed in traditional Thai costume—and he entertained lavishly. Come to think of it, he lived a lot like Ching Wei, minus the Chinese torture shows.

We chatted for a while before dinner, and he made it quite clear that he was a genuine guest there, not part of Ching Wei's captive audience, like the rest of us. He seemed to know everything about my abduction, including the personal vendetta behind it, but he avoided any discussion of his own case.

"Your big mistake was busting Ching Wei for opium back in Chungking. What you should have done was leaned on him and taken a cut of the action. A little moonlighting on the side never hurt anyone, especially in this line of business." He stuck a fresh Salem cigarette into an old ivory holder and demanded a light from a passing servant. Then he put a paternal arm around my shoulder and said, "Come up to my place for dinner sometime, and we can talk in a bit more privacy. I'll send one of my boys around to fetch you."

That evening I also met Ching Wei's personal physician, an eccentric Swiss doctor by the name of Heinrich Hoffmann. He also served as general practitioner for Ching Wei's precious collection of white men. Hoffmann was a big, messy man with a mane of tangled white hair rimming his bald pate. A nicotine-stained mustache drooped over his mouth, and below it hung a gray goatee. He always seemed excited and out of breath, and whenever he spoke a fine spray preceded his words.

Hoffmann was a junkie, so life at Dragon Mountain suited him just fine. Ching Wei shared with him his precious stash of China White—the purest, most potent form of heroin on earth. Usually, the only kind of medical attention Ching Wei ever required from Hoffmann was a fix of his favorite mix whenever the craving hit him.

I ran into Hoffmann again the following week at Moreau's house, where I'd become a frequent visitor. Moreau had fallen off the veranda one evening in a stoned stupor, cutting a deep gash in his forehead that required a dozen stitches. Hoffmann was there to remove the stitches, and afterward he joined Moreau and me for a smoke in the den.

After a few pipes of opium, Hoffmann opened up like a book. "Ching Wei uses about one gram of pure China White per day. If you were to inject that quantity of heroin into a horse, it would kill him instantly."

"So why doesn't it kill Ching Wei?"

"Balance, my dear boy, biochemical balance! The Great Principle of Yin and Yang applied to chemistry." Moreau pressed the pipe to Hoffmann's mouth, and he paused to suck the bowl dry. Plumes of blue smoke hung in wreaths from his snow-white hair. "For every measure of Yin," he continued, visibly warming to his subject, "there must always be an equal but opposite measure of Yang. In cooking, for example, the Chinese use equal measures of sugar and salt in their sauces in order to accent and balance the Yin and Yang flavors. In the case of drugs, the extremely Yin nature of heroin must be balanced within the body with an equal dosage of its own Yang opposite, which, in the case of heroin, is cocaine." He twisted his mustache as he fished for the right words. "When administered together in proper proportions, you may enjoy the profound narcotic euphoria of both drugs without suffering the ill side effects of either. Chemical balance is the key! Due to the presence of two pharmacodynamically opposite drugs in the blood, the body's metabolism does not develop a morbid chemical attachment to either one, and therefore the unpleasant side effects of drug addiction may be easily avoided." Professional pride rang in his voice. "Though in all fairness I must give Ching Wei credit for the original concept, which he derived from the theories of Yin and Yang and Chinese herbal medicine, it is I who discovered that cocaine was the biochemical key to balancing heroin."

"Sorry, Doc, but I don't follow your reasoning. How can you eliminate the bad effects of one narcotic drug by adding to it another equally potent and addictive one? Seems to me that you'd just get twice as polluted."

He shook his head and wagged a bony finger at me. "Not at all. The secret is to determine the correct combination of the two drugs. As long as the body's vital functions and metabolic rate remain in proper balance, all toxins are naturally eliminated from the system. For thousands of years the Chinese have been classifying and prescribing medicinal herbal drugs according to this system of opposite natures. It is part of their ancient pharmacopoeia, and it proves as relevant to modern pharmaceutical science as it does to traditional herbal medicine." He paused again to accept another pipe from Moreau, then continued with renewed energy.

"You should see some of the toxic substances that go into traditional Chinese herbal prescriptions: mercury, lead, cinnabar, arsenic, centipedes, scorpions, datura, graphite, and so forth. All of these items are far more toxic than heroin or cocaine, and yet, by taking them in correct combinations and proper proportions with other drugs of complimentary energies, the patient gains the desired therapeutic benefits without suffering damage to his organs and upsetting his vital functions. Ching Wei first proposed this theory to me many years ago, when his health had begun to deteriorate from excessive dependence on heroin, which he has used for many years to control the pain from the wound in his liver. Ever since I discovered the counterbalancing relationship of cocaine and heroin, he has suffered very little ill effect from his drug habit, even though his daily dosage now far exceeds his former levels."

"Like having your cake and eating it too?"

"Precisely! Now I ask you: what good is having a cake if you cannot eat it too? Dear boy, drugs are God's gift to man, placed at our disposal in their myriad natural forms so that we may discover and use them properly to our benefit. It is the misuse, not the use, of drugs that causes problems, and all of these problems may be avoided simply by following one cardinal rule: never use any drug alone, but only in combination with its own essential opposite."

"I see. Well, one thing I can't stand about opium," I remarked, as Moreau handed me a freshly loaded pipe, "is that it sometimes clogs up my guts for days, especially after smoking two or three days in a row."

"Aha! A perfect example!" Hoffmann declared. "That was

also one of Ching Wei's complaints. Opiates in any form can cause constipation by inhibiting the peristaltic movement of the bowels and rectum. After prolonged use of opiates, the colon and rectal muscles begin to atrophy; peristalsis grows sluggish; and the stomach loses its ability to digest all nutrients except simple sugars. This accounts for the intense craving for sweets displayed by most heroin addicts.

"Cocaine, on the other hand, accelerates peristalsis, stimulates digestion, and tends to evacuate any excess accumulation of waste in the colon. But singular and excessive use of cocaine is just as damaging to the system as heroin, though in a pathologically opposite manner." He sat up and reached for his black bag, pulling out a small vial and a glass syringe. "Please, allow me to demonstrate this principle for you."

"Hold it, Doc! I'll take your word for it. I can't stand needles!"

"Now see here, I am a qualified physician. Intravenous injection is by far the safest and the cleanest method of administering any drug. Smoking and snuffing are not only crude and wasteful by comparison, they also cause untold damage to the lungs and sinuses." He leaned over and peered at my face. "Just as I thought! Your complexion and eyes, as well as the color of your fingernails, tell me that your bowels are stuffed full of excrement, and that, I can assure you, is the most toxic substance of all to the human body. As you Americans like to say, 'You are full of shit!'" He roared with laughter at his own joke and continued to prepare the syringe.

It was true. I hadn't squatted for three or four days, and my gut felt like lead.

"Your condition shall be quickly corrected with proper medication," he said, reaching for my arm. He tied it off with a rubber tube to raise the veins. What the hell, I felt so loaded already from the opium that he could have stuck an ice pick in my arm without me feeling any pain, so I let him slip the needle into my vein and give me a shot of cocaine.

In less than half a minute, I felt the stuff flooding my brain like a wave of cool, clear water. Somehow it felt the way a menthol cigarette tastes—a slight hint of mint in the head. The pleasant sensation spread slowly down to the rest of my body, instantly clearing away the lethargy and heaviness that opium always left in my bones and muscles. When it reached my gut, I felt a depth charge detonate in my bowels. The effects were immediate and explosive. I barely made it to the toilet before my ass erupted with a splash and a roar, dumping out the biggest, foulest pile of shit I'd ever seen in my life. I returned to the den light as a feather, incredibly relieved, and full of energy. I still felt the opium, but the additional presence of cocaine enhanced the feeling tremendously. My mind felt crystal clear.

"That worked great, Doc!" I admitted as I lay back down on my hip. "Moreau, fix me another pipe, old buddy!"

Hoffmann agreed to provide me with a little stash of cocaine from time to time to keep my system balanced during my smoking sessions with Moreau. He also informed me that cocaine was generally not available to the guests at Dragon Mountain. "We must bring it here at great expense all the way from South America. We have tried cultivating coca here, but the soil is not right. Nevertheless, I can spare enough to suffice your needs."

Hoffmann treated himself to a shot of coke, blew another pipe of opium, and told me the story of how he'd met Ching Wei. Like Jim Thompson, Hoffmann wasn't a captive at all: he'd met Ching Wei in Bangkok and become his personal physician there years before coming to Dragon Mountain. A devoted dabbler in drugs, Dr. Hoffmann left his native Zurich amid some sort of scandal there and came to live and work in Bangkok, where recreational drug use is socially acceptable and the raw materials abundantly available.

"One day a patient brought a Chinese lady to my clinic. She was beautiful, elegant—extraordinary! She suffered from chronic insomnia, one of my specialties, and within a month I cured her condition. How? Pharmaceuticals and herbs, Yin and Yang, the best of East and West! My dear boy, you see before you the founder of a new medicine!" He caught his breath, lit a cigarette, and continued.

"Have you ever suffered from insomnia? Terrible affliction! It can make you lose your mind. Needless to say, the lady was profoundly grateful. She invited me to her house for dinner one evening and introduced me to her husband. That was how I met Ching Wei. He expressed deep interest in my work, especially the way I blended Eastern and Western medical theories, and he impressed me with many intelligent questions about chemistry and medicine."

One thing led to another, and before long Hoffmann became Ching Wei's personal physician. Whenever Ching Wei came to Bangkok on business, the two of them met and spent a lot of time together. Before long, Ching Wei put Hoffmann permanently on his payroll, then asked him to quit his Bangkok practice in order to join him up-country. Hoffmann never hesitated.

He designed Ching Wei's first heroin lab, but in those days Ching Wei did not refine heroin for profit. All his profits came from wholesaling raw opium to the Chinese syndicates that refined the stuff into heroin in their own labs hidden along the border between Burma and Thailand. The sole purpose of Ching Wei's lab was for Dr. Hoffmann to research and develop the secret formula for Ching Wei's favorite drug, "China White."

"We do not know how the Chinese do it," Hoffmann sighed. "Of course, they have the advantage of three thousand years of herbal science and alchemy to back up their work. Like us, they start with raw opium, but the purity and potency of the China White they produce far surpasses any other form of heroin in the world, even the very best quality French powder from Marseilles. It is like the difference between the finest champagne and the cheapest beer—both are bubbly and contain alcohol, but the differences in quality and potency, not to mention the effects, are overwhelmingly evident from the first taste. That is why American soldiers returning home from war with heroin habits acquired in Vietnam have caused so much trouble in your country. They search forever but in vain for a drug that gives them the same sensations as the China White they obtained in Vietnam. Their need shall never be satisfied, for no one has yet discovered the secret to producing China White. Many addicts attempt to duplicate its effects with massive doses of ordinary heroin, then die of overdose. Some become desperate criminals; others go mad, or simply kill themselves for relief. You see, another unique feature of China White is that it is so addictive that it is virtually impossible to quit. Prolonged use actually alters the cellular structure of the liver and nervous system. Once addicted, the addict has only two options: continue using China White, or else gradually destroy himself using massive doses of lesser substitutes. And that is why the Chinese developed this formula in the first place—for use as a weapon against your soldiers in Vietnam. Call it 'chemical warfare.'"

"Do the Chinese grow their own opium too?" I figured I may as well milk Hoffmann for some relevant intelligence.

"They grow some in Yunnan, but most of their raw opium comes up from the Burmese Communists in the Kachen Hills up north. The Chinese give them weapons, medicine, and other supplies in exchange for the opium, which they then refine into China White in heroin labs located along the Chinese border with Vietnam. But the Chinese strictly control its distribution, and it never appears for sale on the black market. The only people with access to China White are those to whom the Chinese wish to give access. In order to obtain his supply, Ching Wei must from time to time perform certain favors for the Chinese government, even though he hates Communism with a passion, especially Chinese Communism. To the Chinese, of course, China White is just another commodity, like toothpaste or soap. Each laboratory neatly packages its own variety of China White in vacuum-sealed cellophane parcels and labels it under its own brand name. Ching Wei's personal favorite is 'Snowflake' brand."

"And you're supposed to figure out the formula for making China White so that Ching Wei doesn't have to do favors for the Reds anymore in order to get his supply."

"Correct. He would give anything to discover that formula and rid himself of his dependence on China. That is his political and personal reason. But there is another reason as well, and that is economic. In his hands, China White would revolutionize the entire world's narcotic trade, just as the discovery of ordinary heroin made morphine obsolete overnight. After only one season on the market, China White would eliminate all competitors, and Ching Wei would achieve his long-sought monopoly in the drug trade. Unlike China, Ching Wei has direct access to virtually unlimited quantities of raw opium, and since China White may be produced at about the same cost per gram as ordinary heroin, while yielding a product that is at least one hundred times more potent, the potential for profit is enormous, fantastic! He has been funding my research for years now, in order for me to discover the formula for China White. With that formula in hand, who could stand in his way?"

"Think you'll ever figure it out?"

Hoffmann shrugged. "Frankly, I don't know. It is possible, but very difficult. I have come rather close, but the final stages of the process continue to elude me. In any case, I have my laboratory and all sorts of other interesting drugs to keep me busy in the meantime. There is no hurry. You must come up and visit my bungalow sometime. I can arrange your entry to the palace grounds."

Hoffmann looked up and noticed it had grown dark outside. He quickly packed his bag of tricks and prepared to leave. "I must get back to the palace now. It is almost time for Ching Wei's early evening combination—one part China White with two parts cocaine in a glucose solution. This stimulates his appetite before dinner. The last dose of the evening contains these drugs in opposite proportion to promote restful sleep. Unless," Hoffmann winked lecherously, "he wishes to play with one of his white tigers, in which case I add some additional aphrodisiac extracts to the mix to enhance his potency and prolong his pleasure. Bonsoir, Moreau, and thank you for the fine smoke—you prepare the best pipes in Poong! And try to be more careful—you could easily have fractured your skull in that fall."

"Hold on, Doc. I'll walk back down to the village with you." I suddenly felt famished and did not want to miss dinner at Kiang's. In the past, my smoking sessions with Moreau usually left me without a trace of appetite for food or for sex, but this time, I felt hungry enough to eat a horse, and the weight of an oncoming erection stirred in my pants. Hoffmann's theory seemed to be valid.

After dinner, I discovered that the opium and cocaine cocktail at Moreau's had indeed sharpened my appetite for sex as much as it had for food. Suraya found me rising to her charms like a prize stud, and we went at it like rabbits for hours. That finally sold me on Hoffmann's Yin-Yang dope theory, and that old jingle kept coming to mind: "Things go better with Coke!"

X

Time flew by, and before I knew it, I'd been there for over a year. In the beginning, I'd never been permitted to wander far from the immediate vicinity of Poong, but after a while the sentries grew accustomed to the sight of me, and a few friendly words in Chinese usually got me by their checkpoints for long walks in the hills. An unspoken seniority system prevailed at Dragon Mountain: the longer you stayed there without trying to escape, the greater your freedom to move about and live as you please, as long as you remained well within the boundaries of the domain. Escape attempts always proved fatal.

Ching Wei kept a special squad of U.S. Army Lurps to track down escapees and deserters and to launch punitive raids against his enemies. That's right, Lurps. As you'll recall, that's the name we used in Nam for the acronym LRRP, Long-Range Reconnaissance Patrol—the guys who did all the dirty work for us in that war. This particular squad was on a top-secret mission in northern Laos, when Ching Wei's troops bumped into them while escorting an opium caravan from Burma. Mistaking each other for enemies, the two sides engaged in a wild firefight that ended only when the Lurps finally ran out of ammo two days later. The twelve-man squad inflicted over fifty casualties on Ching Wei's men before they surrendered, losing only one dead and one wounded themselves.

When Ching Wei heard that a dozen men had held off 150 of his own troops for two days, killing or wounding nearly half of them in the action, he was so impressed that he resolved to win their loyalty for himself. At first they were bent on escape, and he had to have them guarded under lock and key round the clock. But after plying them with food, women, and drugs for a while, he finally induced them to stay and settle down there. Their sole condition for cooperating with him was that they be allowed to stay together as a unit and live far apart from the rest of the community.

So Ching Wei gave them their own little fief in a mountainous corner of his domain. He sometimes sent them into rival territories to gather intelligence or terrorize his competitors in the opium trade, but mainly he used them to hunt down deserters and escapees, and to settle personal vendettas with his enemies. They were fanatically loyal to one another and took great pride in their work. Never had they failed to bring back their prey. Ching Wei called them his "hunters," and they enjoyed special privileges at Dragon Mountain, such as the right to bear arms. I'll recount my first meeting with them later.

Meanwhile, Ching Wei kept adding more inmates to his menagerie, and soon there were over a hundred European and American captives in his collection. He kept detailed files on each and every one of us, and whenever the mood struck him to talk about sports or art, to play chess or backgammon, to have a drunken orgy or a serious philosophical discussion, he simply rummaged through his files and sent his guards to fetch the appropriate guests for the occasion. No one ever refused his invitations.

His domain covered an area about one hundred miles wide east to west and one hundred fifty miles long north to south. Most of it lay within Burma's mountainous Shan Plateau, though corners of it spilled over into Laos and northern Thailand. His forces, which he referred to as the "Shan Freedom Army," held sway over the entire Golden Triangle, and from his headquarters at Dragon Mountain he controlled—directly or indirectly—over 80 percent of the opium trafficking in the region. His stronghold was impenetrable by land, and rumor had it that he kept a few Soviet surface-to-air missiles planted on top of the mountain above his palace, just in case anyone tried to attack him by air. The missiles came out of Laos, stolen for him by the Lurps.

The first time I managed to get beyond the outskirts of Poong was to attend a soccer game in another village with Hoffmann and Moreau. Ching Wei was a great soccer fan and had organized a league among his captives. Except for the monsoon season and the opium harvests, matches took place regularly once a month, and Ching Wei rarely missed them. The games were held in a village about three miles northwest of Poong.

"He organizes the teams along national lines," Hoffmann explained as we strolled to the match. "Today France will play against England, and I wager that the French will win both the match and the championship this year. Last year the Americans won, but only because they had so many players from which to select a strong team. This year Ching Wei has been collecting more Europeans, and their teams have improved considerably as a result."

"What's the prize for winning the championship?" Knowing Ching Wei, he'd offer a mouthwatering Pavlovian reward for the winner just to sharpen the competition.

"The winning team enjoys three days and three nights of unbridled debauchery in special guest bungalows within the palace grounds. Each player on the winning team also receives three extra months of rations from the provisions shop."

As the jungle gradually cleared, giving way to paddies and vegetable patches, the village appeared in the distance. The land around the village was neatly terraced for rice cultivation, but beyond the village all of the hills and valleys were carpeted with red and purple poppies in full bloom, their blossoms shimmering in the sunlight.

The village was much smaller and more primitive than Poong, except for a perfectly manicured, full-sized soccer field.

The stands were nearly full when we arrived, and a large scoreboard displayed the French and British flags, indicating the teams that day. Ching Wei and his rambling entourage of Asian women, white guests, and Chinese bodyguards occupied a plush private box at centerfield. I noticed Jim Thompson among them.

It was just like attending a soccer match anywhere else in the world. Each team had its own distinctive uniform and colors. Vendors milled through the stands selling roasted peanuts, fresh fruit, lemon water, and rice beer, and the crowd went wild with every goal. France won, 4-2.

Over the next few months, I visited several other villages as well. Everywhere it was the same story: dozens of white men foisted upon local families as wards for life, or until they induced the barbarians to marry and settle down with one of their daughters. There was always the usual assortment of newcomers still puffed up with pride and dreams of escape, old-timers with large local families and comfortable homes of their own, hopeless derelicts completely given over to opium or arack, all of them part and parcel of Ching Wei's motley menagerie.

I fared better than most. For one thing, I lived in Poong, which was by far the most comfortable village, with ready access to the store and bar. For another, my vital role as pilot entitled me to far more rations from the store than I needed as a single man, so I used most of my coupons to pick up stuff for Kiang's household, which made life there all the more cozy. Locals were not permitted to trade at the shop.

Eventually the inevitable happened: Suraya got pregnant. Frankly, I was surprised it hadn't happened earlier. I think she'd been using some sort of herbal birth control, because she often drank a bitter brew the morning after we made love. It was only after she stopped drinking that concoction that she got pregnant.

By that time we communicated fairly well with her pidgin English and my broken Shan. "Have baby coming," she told me, rubbing her distended belly. "You wanting boy, wanting girl?"

"Make it a girl," I said, "and make her as beautiful as you."

"Okay, girl can do," she said, "I tell Buddha." Every day she burned incense and prayed for a girl at the family altar, and by

God, when the time came, she produced a beautiful little girl. Though technically she did not qualify for Dr. Hoffmann's services unless I formally married her, he delivered the baby for us anyway. We named her Shana.

The issue of marriage came up more than once between us, especially after the baby was born. Suraya wanted us to get married, have more babies, and build a house of our own up in the hills overlooking the village, just like any woman who stays with the same man long enough to bear his children. But every time she brought it up, I refused her, because I felt I couldn't marry another woman while I still had a wife of my own back home in San Francisco. To me it was a matter of principle, but to her it didn't make a damn bit of difference that I already had another wife.

"Never mind!" she'd say, grabbing my crotch. "You big man, need two wife. Me number two wife, never mind, OK!"

Had I granted her wish, Ching Wei would have built us a nice big house of our own on a hill outside the village, but at the time I still clung stubbornly to Western values and refused. So she and I and the baby continued living together at her family's house in Poong, much to my everlasting regret.

XI

*You are cordially invited
to celebrate
the Year of the Wood Tiger
at the Palace of the Green Dragon*
Friday 6:00 PM
Chinese attire required

So read the invitation delivered to me by a palace guard three days before the Chinese Lunar New Year in January 1974. It was stamped with Ching Wei's personal seal, enclosed in a bright red envelope, and embossed with a golden tiger. "Green Dragon" was one of Ching Wei's many self-anointed nicknames, derived from the Taoist mythology of the White Tiger and Green Dragon.

Ching Wei observed all the traditional Chinese festivals—Lantern Festival, Dragon Boat Festival, Mid-Autumn Moon Festival—but by far the biggest celebration of the year was Chinese New Year. On New Year's Eve, he always held a big banquet at the palace for his senior officers and favorite foreign guests, and on New Year's Day he held court in his throne room, while every village sawbwa, every white guest, and every Chinese officer in his domain came forth to pay respects with a formal *kowtow* and a token gift. That's the Chinese tradition. In return, he presented each of his well-wishers with a little red envelope stuffed with "lucky money" to start off the new year on an auspicious note.

So on New Year's Eve I trimmed my beard, donned my Chinese robe, and hiked up the path to the palace. The main gate was festooned with fresh flowers and strips of red paper bearing lucky messages in elegant Chinese calligraphy. I flashed my invitation card at a guard, and he escorted me through the garden into the courtyard. From there a girl in red silk took me up to the throne room, where Ching Wei stood chatting and drinking champagne with his guests.

"Ah, Happy New Year, Captain Jack!" Ching Wei greeted me with a big grin as I entered the room. "Have some champagne." I took a glass and toasted him. "Come, I wish to show you my New Year gift to myself."

He led me to the other side of the room, where an enormous electronic console occupied the entire wall. It looked like the cockpit of a spaceship, with all sorts of dials and gauges, switches and relays, audiovisual equipment, amplifiers, modulators, and a row of six large television screens. Familiar Chinese love songs from Taiwan played on the tape deck.

"Please be seated. Instead of the usual entertainment, which is not appropriate on this lucky day, I have decided to amuse you with my new audiovisual center. Mr. Wellington has installed it for me at a cost of over one hundred thousand American dollars." Everyone gave Todd a hearty round of applause, and we all felt relieved to be spared the spectacle of another bizarre torture.

Ching Wei fiddled with the dials—a child playing with his new toy—and suddenly all six screens flashed to life. The two in the center displayed programs in full color. One received Bangkok broadcasts through a large radar dish placed high on the mountain, while the other was connected to a video recorder to show movies.

The other four screens flashed black-and-white images from four video cameras rigged at strategic points around his domain. One scanned the village square in Poong; another was trained on the soccer field in the next village; and the other two displayed scenes unfamiliar to me, probably distant check posts along his security network. Ching Wei demonstrated how the cameras could be remotely controlled from the console to zoom in for close-up shots.

"From now on, when I do not feel like attending in person, I can watch the soccer games from the comfort of my own parlor. I can also observe the behavior of my guards on duty at even the most remote posts. And I can keep in close contact with events around the world through the Bangkok news broadcasts. I am very pleased indeed!"

He showed us a few more functions, such as a shortwave radio capable of picking up police and military communications throughout the region, intercoms that connected him with every guard post, and a computer to be used for business purposes. Then he switched the whole system off and announced, "Now, gentlemen, let us proceed to the dining room and sit down to eat."

The banquet table was lavishly set for twenty-four guests, the silverware and crystal sparkling in the warm glow of dozens of red candles. Ching Wei sat at the head of the table, with Hoffmann at the other end. The rest of us arranged ourselves along both sides. Ching Wei clapped his hands, and out came six stunning serving girls, naked as the day they were born, all of them bona fide white tigers. Everyone at the table gaped, and Ching Wei looked immensely pleased.

Despite his depraved habits, Ching Wei was a gracious and generous host, and no one could fault him for his hospitality. Perhaps it was his way of compensating us for our lost freedom, but more than that, I think he just enjoyed entertaining. He really got a kick watching his guests get stinking drunk and enjoy themselves, and no matter how ridiculous the conversation became, he always listened to everyone with sincere interest. We served as his primary source of entertainment, and as sounding boards for whatever far-fetched ideas he might have in mind.

"You know what you must do next, Ching Wei?" a German named Hermann said through a mouthful of braised wild peacock. Next to Americans, Ching Wei liked Germans best. "You must install a powerful television transmitter here and beam your dinner parties directly into Red China—live and in full color! Let the masses see for themselves how well you have done here as a free-enterprising capitalist roader!" Hermann's vast gut heaved as he roared with laughter.

"An excellent suggestion!" Ching Wei replied, selecting a steamed quail's egg and placing it on Hermann's plate.

"And how about that new computer you just showed us?" said Jim Slater, an American computer technician from Singapore who'd been kidnapped while on holiday in Chiang Mai. "I could program your entire operation for you, top to bottom. You could pull out any information you need with a simple push of a button." He gave a rapturous account of the wonders of modern computer technology. Desperate for a chance to work with his beloved computers again, Slater pleaded his case. But Ching Wei was way ahead of him.

"I have already ordered the most recent catalogs and manuals for what you call 'software.' When the information arrives, I will summon you to further discuss these plans." Slater looked elated and toasted Ching Wei.

The girls kept streaming in with steaming platters of succulent Chinese delicacies, most of it specially prepared for the New Year with the costliest ingredients available. I remember having braised elephant trunk, stewed monkey paw, sautéed bird tongues, and at least a dozen different varieties of wild bird eggs. It was a party that lived up to Ching Wei's own name—a "Great Celebration."

After dinner, we retired to the throne room and sat around the new electronic console to watch a Chinese kung-fu movie broadcast in Thai from Bangkok. I found myself far more attracted by the advertisements than the movie. Somehow those corny ads with their silly jingles made me feel nostalgic for the outside world, a sentiment I hadn't felt for quite some time.

"Come, it is almost midnight," Ching Wei beckoned us to the door after the movie was over. "Let us go outside and enjoy the fireworks. We Chinese invented fireworks, you know?" At the stroke of midnight on Lunar New Year's Eve, Chinese throughout the world ignite tons of firecrackers, Roman candles, sky rockets, and other explosive devices in order to frighten evil spirits away from their homes and communities, thereby assuring an auspicious beginning to the new year.

We gathered in the courtyard, and when the clock struck twelve, a racket erupted that echoed back and forth over hill and dale, rumbling like thunder through the forests of Ching Wei's kingdom. Rockets blazed into the sky, cleaving the darkness with phosphorescent trails, then exploding in dazzling showers of light. It looked like the Fourth of July.

But suddenly something went wrong. As the first burst of fireworks faded away, more ominous sounds came to the fore. Frightened screams and angry shouts floated up from Poong as a new round of explosions pierced the night. No doubt about it—what we now heard was the clatter of machine guns and the crump of grenades, not fireworks.

Ching Wei knew it instantly. "Everyone back inside!" he bellowed. "Quickly!" A guard raced across the courtyard and whispered urgently in his ear.

As our confused party huddled in the throne room, Ching Wei announced in a merry voice, "Well, gentlemen, it seems that my old comrade in arms Colonel Hsu has taken this opportunity to send me his own New Year's greetings. His men have just attacked the main village in Poong and are coming this way. Dr. Hoffmann, Captain Robertson, Mr. Wellington, you three follow me. The rest of you wait here until this is over. You will be safe."

He tapped a panel behind his throne, and a section of wall slid open, revealing a narrow stone stairwell. We rushed up the steps behind Ching Wei just as the first grenade rocked the courtyard outside.

XII

The stairs led up to a chamber chiseled into solid rock high above the throne room. Racks with guns of every description covered the walls from floor to ceiling. Bandoliers, banana clips, and crates of ammo were stacked against the walls. Steel panels covered three small, horizontal windows cut into the wall facing the outside.

Due to the commotion, I hadn't noticed that six of Ching Wei's bodyguards had bounded up the steps behind us, fully armed. They secured the door to the stairwell and stood in silent sentry, awaiting further orders.

"Now let us see what is going on out there," Ching Wei said. He reached for a switch to dim the lights, which were powered by a battery pack rather than the central generator. He ordered a guard to crank open the center window panel, and a stiff breeze immediately blew in the sharp smell of cordite and the staccato chatter of automatic gunfire.

The chamber was perched high above the courtyard, carved into the solid stone cliff that soared above the palace. Secure as an eagle's nest, it commanded a sweeping view of the entire village and surrounding hills, and it was stocked with sufficient provisions to last several months. Far below, the flash of gunfire in the village looked like fireflies flitting through the night.

Dr. Hoffmann, already quite drunk when the shooting started, slumped sullenly against a wall and slid to the floor, his evening ruined. "At least we should have brought up a few bottles of champagne," he complained.

"Shut up!" Ching Wei snapped, rushing over to the gun racks. He grabbed a long rifle of German design, mounted with a large scope, then ran back to the window to scan the landscape through the lens. "Just as I thought," he announced. "Those are Colonel Hsu's troops down there. Look!"

He stepped aside and let me shoulder the rifle. It was mounted for night vision with a Starlite scope, which rendered the entire landscape visible in remarkable detail. A vicious firefight was raging in and around Poong, with Ching Wei's troops rallying to keep the invaders from approaching the palace. I could see clearly that both sides were Chinese.

Ching Wei grabbed the rifle from me, took careful aim through the scope, and commenced firing. Like a kid in a pinball arcade, he cheered himself on with every hit and cursed bitterly at every miss. He was having a ball.

"Please join me in the fun, Jack," he suggested, pausing to snap a fresh clip into the magazine. "There are two more rifles on the wall equipped for night vision. Help yourself."

I reached for a rifle, and a guard cranked open a second window panel for me. But I was not interested in target practice that night. I was worried sick about Suraya and Shana. I scanned the village for a glimpse of Kiang's house, but it was hidden behind the foliage. I could see Moreau's veranda up on the hill beyond the village, but there were no signs of movement there. Moreau probably lay there smoking opium and snoozing through the entire attack.

The battle waxed and waned until dawn, but it was impossible to tell from there who had the upper hand. At one point Ching Wei sent Hoffmann clambering down the stairs with two guards to fetch his medical bag. When he returned, he was so out of breath that it took him about half an hour to calm down enough to mix the drugs, fix the syringe, and administer a shot to Ching Wei. The moment the plunger pumped the solution into his vein, Ching Wei's tension and fatigue melted away like ice in the sun, and that smug smirk spread across his face again. He ran back to the window and continued firing up a storm. Exhausted and hungover, Hoffmann slouched on the floor and took a shot of his own.

By dawn, the gunfire had grown sporadic, and by the time the sun rose through the trees, all was quiet again down below. Birds sang out their morning songs, and cicadas droned in the trees, as if nothing had happened.

"They have gone," Ching Wei said. A pile of empty brass clattered around his ankles as he stepped away from the window and replaced the rifle on the rack. The reek of gunpowder was overwhelming. "Hsu is a fool to invade Dragon Mountain! This is a clear sign of his growing desperation. He must be dealt with severely and soon!"

Ching Wei barked a command, and his guards jumped to life. They unbarred the door to let us out, then dragged Hoffmann to his feet and helped him down the steps.

Out in the courtyard, debris was scattered everywhere. There were several jagged craters from grenades lobbed over the wall, but the palace itself had not been breached. An officer ran in and reported that the attackers had retreated back into the jungle and were gone. Since the coast was clear, I left Ching Wei at the palace and hurried down to the village.

Beyond the main wall, just outside the gate, bodies were scattered all over the place. A big pile of corpses lay strewn just outside the palace gates, stiff as boards but without any sign of visible wounds. They'd dropped dead in their tracks from some kind of lethal gas sprayed at them from the gates by Ching Wei's troops.

Further down the trail, I passed another gruesome scene. A dozen bodies were literally blown to bits, chunks of flesh and bone splattered against the rocks and trees. These were the victims of Todd's sophisticated booby traps, which Ching Wei had detonated by remote control from his gunroom.

But the worst carnage had occurred in the village.

When I emerged from the trees and entered the village square, all I saw was death and destruction everywhere. The village was a smoldering ruin of splintered timbers, charred thatch, and scattered rubble. The store had been looted and torched, and the big communal pavilion was reduced to a pile of dust and debris. Bodies and torn limbs lay askew all over the place, many of them cut to ribbons by machine-gun fire and grenade shrapnel. The only things left standing were the ancient bodhi trees.

A hard lump floated up from my gut to my gullet, and I began trembling with premonition. I tried to shake off the terrible feeling as I approached Kiang's house, but it kept brewing inside.

When I saw the house—or what was left of it—my whole gut heaved. The entire roof had collapsed, and only a few timbers remained intact. The lovely garden where Suraya and I had spent so many happy times together was trampled and torn to shreds. The most pathetic sobbing I'd ever heard greeted me as I walked up the path to the house. Rocking rhythmically on her haunches just inside the threshold, Kiang's eldest daughter wailed over the mangled corpses of her mother and father, their faces shot up beyond recognition.

She looked up when I touched her shoulder, tears streaming down her cheeks, too overcome with grief to utter a single word. She just shook her head sadly and continued sobbing.

In the front room, I found the body of the youngest sister, naked and twisted grotesquely in the wreckage. She'd been raped before having her throat cut from ear to ear.

With feet of lead, I stepped over her corpse and entered the little room in back that had been my home for the past three years. Crumpled on our cot in a bloody heap I saw Suraya, her hand still clutching a machete and her body riddled with bullet holes. At her feet lay a dead Chinese, his chest cut open from collarbone to sternum.

I flung him aside and gathered her into my arms. Her body was still warm. Then I heard a muffled cry. Nestled securely on the cot beneath her mother's breast I found little Shana, burbling and blinking at me with recognition. If it hadn't been for the baby, I think I would have gone crazy with grief and run amok into the jungle.

    The next day I buried Suraya in a quiet meadow up by a mountain stream, where we'd often gone to fish, pick herbs, and make love. Then I had the village sawbwa perform a posthumous wedding ceremony for us, an ancient Shan tradition whereby the soul of a departed lover is united forever in spiritual matrimony with the surviving partner. It broke my heart to think that if only I'd agreed to marry her earlier, as she'd so often pleaded for, we would have built our own house high up on a hill beyond the village, and she would not have been in Poong that night . . .

**United States of America
Central Intelligence Agency
Bangkok**

To: Director/Covert, Langley, Virginia
Re: Operation Burma Road
Class: CONFIDENTIAL
Date: February 28, 1981

After recounting the events that resulted in the death of his adopted family, Captain Robertson exhibited signs of extreme emotional distress, so we have allowed him two days of rest under sedation before completing his debriefing. A copy of the entire transcript will be forwarded to your office in the next embassy pouch.

We are trying to verify a few key facts in order to authenticate Robertson's story. According to Bangkok police files, an expatriate Frenchman named Moreau did, in fact, disappear while living in Thailand in 1968. Interpol conducted a brief investigation at the request of French authorities, but they turned up nothing and dropped the matter.

We have also established the fact that a Swiss national by the name of Dr. Heinrich Hoffmann was registered as a foreign resident in Bangkok for nearly ten years, but no one seems to recall when he left or where he went. We have not been able to trace anyone by the name of Todd Wellington in Thailand or Laos, but there are records of someone by that name living in Singapore until 1970.

The most intriguing aspect of the transcript as far as our own office is concerned is the reference to Jim Thompson. Until his sudden disappearance while vacationing with friends in the Cameron Highlands in Malaysia in 1967, Thompson was our main man for covert operations at our Bangkok station. We never turned up a single clue to explain his disappearance, so we finally closed the case in 1975. Robertson's testimony, if true, explains everything.

We also checked out the so-called "Lurps" mentioned by Robertson. Most of the Long-Range Reconnaissance Patrols (LRRP) sent into Laos were six-man recon squads, but the unit referred to by Robertson was a twelve-man combat team. We've discovered, however, that a twelve-man combat team was, in fact, sent into Laos during that time frame to knock out a Soviet missile pad there. They never returned. Apparently quite a few LRRP squads disappeared into the jungle and were never seen again during the Vietnam War, but due to the covert nature of their missions—especially in Laos, where we were not legally sanctioned to operate—these losses were never formally acknowledged by Army Command. They were simply listed as Missing in Action, and they still are. We suggest you follow this up through MIA and POW records in Washington.

As far as this character Ching Wei is concerned, you already have on file all the information we've managed to collect on him over the years, but it doesn't amount to much. Most of our information about him is hearsay, and we've never even come close to catching him, although army records confirm what Robertson told us about his activities in China during World War II. Our contacts in Thai intelligence have not been very helpful on this—they deny any knowledge of his involvement in illegal activities, which means they've been well paid to protect his interests. And the Burmese authorities refuse to even discuss his case with us. Obviously he's very well connected on both sides. According to all accounts, he is perfectly capable of the extravagance and perversity attributed to him by Robertson.

From the evidence we have gathered so far, we have no reason to doubt any aspect of Robertson's story. We are continuing to investigate details of the case, and we will forward any new findings to your office in the next dispatch.

XIII

Everything changed after that. Colonel Hsu's rude New Year attack not only enraged Ching Wei, it also amplified his paranoia, and Dragon Mountain began to feel more like the camp of armed bandits that it really was, rather than the rustic tribal community it seemed to be.

Ching Wei was utterly furious that his defense network had been breached. Hsu's troops had broken through a key checkpoint when the guards on duty there, unable to resist the merry celebrations in the village, had briefly abandoned their posts shortly before midnight in order to go watch the fireworks and grab a share of the food and drink in Poong. True to his stated policy, Ching Wei exterminated every guard responsible for the breach of security, as well as every member of their families. All were tortured and killed in the most painful manner possible by the Black Dragons, and every troop in Ching Wei's domain was ordered to attend the executions as a lesson in vigilance and obedience.

After burying Suraya, I helped Kiang's surviving daughter to repair the house sufficiently to keep the weather out, but I could no longer bear to sleep there at night. The memories—

and the vivid dreams they evoked—were too painful. Everything there reminded me of her, and the house echoed with her frequent pleas that we get married and move into our own house outside Poong. How could I stay there with that on my mind?

With Ching Wei's permission, Shana and I moved into Moreau's house, where we found a warm welcome. Besides, there were no houses left intact in Poong to serve as alternate "guest" quarters for me, and since I was required to live within Ching Wei's beck and call, Moreau's place was the only viable option. He and his wife Loma treated us like part of their own family, and their generous hospitality gradually revived my spirits. Loma washed my clothes and always set a place for me at their table. Their daughter became a live-in playmate for Shana, who was still too young to realize what had happened to her mother. To express my gratitude, I helped Loma with the garden and the housework while Moreau went to work in Ching Wei's orchid garden, and I did a lot of the shopping and other chores for her as well.

Shortly after moving in with Moreau, I got another invitation for dinner at Jim Thompson's house. He'd had me up there a few times before to attend his dinner parties, but always in the company of other guests, so we hadn't had a chance to talk much. This time I was the only one invited.

His servant came to pick me up one afternoon, and I followed him beyond the village to the lake, where Thompson's house stood amid a lush Chinese garden. It was an exact replica of his mansion in Bangkok—even the Buddhist statuary in the garden was the same as before.

Jim greeted me in the hallway, dressed in a flamboyant red silk kimono and straw sandals, a cigarette burning in his ever-present ivory holder. "Good to see you, Jack. Would have invited you back sooner, but Hsu's little panty raid put a damper on things around here for a while." He led me into the living room and poured me a Russian vodka. He even had ice.

It was wary small talk for a while, but a few stiff drinks finally loosened us both up. Funny how this line of work always keeps you on guard, even when you're supposed to be relaxing with friends.

"You've done all right for yourself," I remarked, openly admiring his house and art collection. "Not easy on Company pay."

"No, it's not," he laughed. "But two and a half million bucks worth of gold bullion should last me quite a while, don't you think?" He got up and started pacing the floor as he spoke, sucking smoke from his ivory holder. "I did my fair share for the Company, Jack, just like we all did. Never once steered them wrong, and never gave an inch to the other side. I'm not the Kim Philby type.

"But I learned early in the game to keep my options open. If guys like us don't take the initiative to feather our own nests while we still have the chance, we end up staying out in the cold until someone comes along and pops us, or else we get sent back to a dull desk job in Washington, and who the hell wants that?"

"So you did some moonlighting on the side?"

"Yup. I first met Ching Wei through Dr. Hoffmann, whom I knew in the old days back in Bangkok. Ching Wei and I socialized a bit whenever he was in town, and his wife there bought all her silk in my shop. From the very start, we both recognized the potential benefits in our relationship. One thing led to another—you know how it goes—and by 1962 I was helping Ching Wei move his dope out of Thailand. Company connections made it simple to grease the right palms in those days, and I myself never saw or touched the stuff. I just took a nice fat cut off the top in the form of gold bullion. Where the dope went, or to whom, I never knew and never asked. Everything was very discreet and low-key then. That was back when Ching Wei was still a minor player and Colonel Hsu was the main operator in the Golden Triangle."

"Before the fiasco with General Rammakone in 1965?"

"Right. That incident really fucked things up. It took Ching Wei almost two years to recover from that, but he bounced back stronger than ever and eventually supplanted Hsu as the kingpin. We had just gotten our operation back into swing again, when some rookie Thai customs agent accidentally uncovered the scam and tried to earn himself a promotion by reporting it. What he earned was an early trip to the grave, but by then it was too late. The cat was out of the bag.

"Fortunately, the rookie's supervisor was on Ching Wei's payroll, and he tipped me off in time. I packed up my gold and most of my precious antiques and had it all trucked up to Chiang Mai, where Ching Wei's boys picked it up and brought it here to Dragon Mountain. Then I closed up shop and took off for a little holiday with some friends in Malaysia." He chuckled at how easy it had been. "One afternoon I went out for my usual stroll in the forest and just kept walking. And here I am! I was amazed by all the publicity my disappearance generated. Rather flattering, really."

"Two and a half million bucks in gold! Not bad, Jim."

"Sure beats the three hundred eighty thousand in paper money that you squirreled away in Hong Kong. Fat lot of good that does you now!" He laughed at my surprise. "Ching Wei showed me his file on you a long time ago. You'd be amazed how much he knows. Nasty of him to threaten your son in Taipei, but that's the name of the game."

Compared to Jim, I felt like a small-time crook. All I'd ever done was accept some gifts and a few bribes for turning my head the other way when certain things, or people, were stowed in my cargo bay. I also dabbled a bit in precious gems and currency exchange, but I never dealt in dope. Maybe I should have joined Ching Wei as a silent partner long ago, back in Chungking, instead of being such a straight arrow.

"Only difference between selling dope and selling favors, Jack, is that you make a lot more money selling dope. And the only reward you get for being straitlaced in this business is a poke in the eye with a sharp stick. You should have gone for the big bucks years ago and retired, like me."

"So it seems." But I had another question in mind now, and only he could answer it. "Tell me, Jim, does Ching Wei know about Burma Road?" Jim would have been privy to those plans because we first laid them out in 1966, a year before he disappeared.

"Nope—at least not from me. Like I said, I've never betrayed Company business. But I can tell you this much: he's got an inkling that something fishy is going on. He's received a few reports that the CIA is trying to establish a network of direct contacts with the Bur-Com and other insurgent groups up north, and he doesn't like it one bit, but he has no idea that you were involved in that. Right now, he's the only thing standing between the Communists up north and the heartland of Burma down south, and that's the big ace up his sleeve. As long as he keeps sending the heads of rebel leaders down to Rangoon in baskets, the government will never move against him. But if the CIA establishes direct contacts up here and negotiates a political settlement between the insurgent groups and Rangoon, Ching Wei loses all his own political clout, and the central government will close in on him. You're damn lucky he doesn't know you're involved in Burma Road. If he knew that it was you who'd been organizing a network of contacts around here, he'd have every single name squeezed out of you like water from a sponge by those barbaric Black Dragon bodyguards of his. I really detest those animals! Fortunately for you, his interest in you is strictly personal, not political."

We had a few more drinks and talked about old times, then sat down to an excellent dinner of classical Thai cuisine—his favorite fare. All of his servants were Thai—most of them from his old household in Bangkok—and he always addressed them fluently in their own language. If he had a boyfriend there, as the rumor went, he didn't introduce him to me. After cognac, cigars, and another long chat out on the terrace, he sent a servant to escort me back down to Poong.

I saw Jim a few more times after that at some of Ching Wei's parties, but he never invited me up to his place again. He didn't want to get too close to someone who'd been an enemy of Ching Wei, especially an old Company crony like me. It wouldn't look right. He had his own circle of friends, and for kicks he sometimes accompanied Ching Wei incognito on business trips to Bangkok and other Asian cities. He told me that he'd even joined Ching Wei on one of his visits to Taipei, posing as a garment buyer.

In any case, Jim suffered a stroke in 1975, and I never saw him again after that. Hoffmann told me the stroke left Jim half paralyzed and unable to speak. He continued to live in his villa like a vegetable in a hothouse, attended by his entourage of Thai servants, until his death in 1978.

XIV

One of the first things I did after settling in at Moreau's place was to revive my long-neglected regimen of Chinese martial arts and Taoist breathing exercises. Once upon a time they'd been second nature to me—as routine as eating and sleeping—but ever since my abduction I'd done nothing to stay in shape.

After losing Suraya, I sank into such a deep funk of depression that I no longer gave a damn about anything, and apathy was becoming a way of life for me. But gradually, thanks to Moreau's opium pipe and Loma's tender loving care, my spirits revived and I began to recall some of the lessons Old Lee had taught me back in Chungking.

"The Seven Emotions," he explained, "are love, hate, joy, sorrow, anger, fear, and desire. In excess, any one of these emotions disrupts our inner spiritual harmony. Like powerful drugs, strong emotions provide a brief burst of energy and the illusion of relief, while confusing the mind and damaging the internal organs. Eventually, both body and mind become addicted to this self-indulgence, and the energy imbalance it produces disrupts the entire system, just as chronic use of drugs does. The tyranny of emotional excess can only be eliminated through the proper cultivation of spirit. Spirit alone has the power to harness the emotions, harmonize energy, and restore the natural functions of the vital organs."

At first it took a lot of effort, but soon I resumed a regular daily regimen of exercise and meditation. Each day at the crack of dawn, I started with an hour of deep breathing and stretching exercises out in the garden. Before lunch I practiced another hour of basic martial art forms, followed by a complete round of tai chi. It took six months of daily practice for me to regain complete control of my breath and expand my lungs and diaphragm to full capacity again, and the improvement in my health was immediate and amazing. After only a few weeks, I felt as if a heavy wet blanket had been lifted from my spirit. I stopped talking to myself. Flowers smelled good again, and my appetite grew. Instead of moping around my room all day, I started going out on long exploratory hikes in the hills again.

And as my health improved, so did my libido. It wasn't long before Moreau's wife and I were making eyes at each other.

Although I still smoked opium from time to time with Moreau, I followed Dr. Hoffmann's advice and never smoked the stuff without taking a bit of cocaine along with it. Hoffmann supplied enough for my needs, which didn't amount to much, but instead of injecting it as he suggested, I simply snuffed it. It worked fine. Thanks to the coke, I never again got constipated, short of breath, or groggy from smoking opium, and neither drug affected my exercise program. I tried like hell to get Moreau to balance his heavy opium habit with some cocaine, but he stubbornly refused to change his ways and continued wasting away. I don't think he wanted to lift the fog. He preferred total oblivion.

I bumped into Hoffmann one morning while shopping at the store, and he invited me to visit his house. "Come up to my place for dinner tonight," he suggested. "I'll show you my laboratory." I was curious to see how "the other half" lived—those privileged few with private bungalows within the palace compound—and accepted his invitation. Hoffmann was the only white man permitted to live within the palace grounds; all the other residents were ranking Chinese officers and technicians, and, of course, Ching Wei's retinue of women and servants.

We met at the bar that afternoon and had a few beers before heading up the mountain. Hoffmann's familiar face and stern air of authority got me by the guards at the gate with no questions asked. As I followed him down a meandering garden path, I noticed the tiled roofs and stone walls of various villas poking through the trees and bamboo groves. They all looked spacious and comfortable, and unlike the benighted village below, each was fed electricity from a power line connected to the central generator beneath the palace. The grounds stretched far and wide and were exquisitely landscaped throughout, with charming grottos, ornate pavilions, and dreamy lotus ponds.

"The wall enclosing this compound is almost two kilometers long," Hoffmann informed me. "Ching Wei's palace is located in the center," he swept his hand around, "and our houses are scattered among the gardens. There are now fifteen villas, but more are under construction. Ah, here is my place now."

He turned off the main path and followed a flagstone walkway up to a set of mossy steps that passed through a round moon gate. We entered a miniature Chinese garden and crossed a little stone bridge over a carp pond. A path of smooth flat stones zigzagged up to the house. Hoffmann pushed open the door, kicked off his shoes, and stepped into a pair of soft leather slippers, indicating for me to do the same.

"Lulu, Liebling, I'm home," he shouted down the hall. He motioned me into a rattan chair and offered me a choice of brandy, vodka, or wine. "We even have ice," he noted.

"Vodka on the rocks, with a twist," I replied.

"Rocks I know; that means ice. But what is this 'twist'? Is that not a popular American dance?"

I nearly burst a gut laughing, the first real belly laugh I'd enjoyed for months. Having lived in the jungle since the mid-1960s, the only "twist" Hoffmann recalled was the one Chubby Checker made famous.

"'Twist' means a slice of lemon peel twisted into a drink," I explained. "American bar slang."

"Yes, I see, certainly. Very logical. We do indeed have a 'twist' for you." He disappeared briefly, returning with my drink and a glass of wine for himself. "We are fortunate this evening. A guard shot two monkeys this morning and has exchanged them with my wife for half a bottle of brandy. There is nothing I like better than wild monkey prepared the Chinese way, braised in rice wine with ginseng and ginger. But come, let me show you around."

The house was built in traditional Chinese style, a square, two-story structure with an open courtyard in the middle, to which every room on the ground floor gave access. The floors were polished teak planks, and the furniture was rattan and lacquered Chinese hardwood.

"Here we are," he announced, "my pride and joy. This is where I spend most of my time when not attending Ching Wei." He unlocked a heavy, steel-banded door, and we entered his lab.

It looked like a scene from one of those old Frankenstein movies. There were bell jars, test tubes, and potbellied flasks, all connected by an intricate maze of rubber tubing, glass pipes, and electric wires. Microscopes, meters, cabinets full of chemicals, electronic gadgets, experimental animals gazing forlornly from their cages—the whole works were there. All that was missing was a monster strapped to the table.

"Actually, Ching Wei has three Chinese chemists working in another laboratory in the compound, and there are two more labs located near the Thai border. But they are all engaged in commercial heroin production, not research. Only I have my own private research laboratory. It was built exactly to my specifications, with the express purpose of discovering the secret of China White."

"But I thought Ching Wei dealt only in bulk raw opium, not in heroin."

"Ach, that is nonsense! Better to say that the 'bulk' of his business is raw opium—about three hundred tons per year to be precise. But he refines about one hundred tons of that to produce ten tons of commercial heroin in those laboratories. The market value of ten tons of pure heroin is at least ten times greater than that of a hundred tons of raw opium."

"So why does he always deny engaging in heroin trafficking?" I knew I was in for another lesson in Chinese logic.

"Public relations, dear boy, and politics. And, of course, 'face.' You see, Ching Wei is a true crusader against Communism. He calls his own forces the Shan Freedom Army, and he claims to represent the interests of the Shan tribesmen here, who have been fighting for autonomy from Burma ever since the British left this region after World War II. And in fact, he does actively support the cause of Shan independence, which naturally makes him a great hero in the eyes of the Shan tribes who produce his opium and protect his kingdom. But his official position as far as the outside world is concerned is that he taxes the opium caravans that pass through his territory in order to finance his campaigns against Communist rebels in northern Burma and Thailand, and that makes him a big hero to central government authorities in Rangoon and Bangkok, who in return do not interfere in his affairs up here and protect him from those meddlesome Americans. Indeed, he launches frequent raids against Communist encampments, and you have seen for yourself what he does to Communist agents captured by his men. If he catches officers or cadres, he always sends their heads down to Rangoon in baskets. He detests Communism in any form, and both the Thai and Burmese governments are most grateful for his efforts."

"So they leave him alone."

"The authorities simply turn a blind eye to his opium business—for a handsome share of the profits, of course. In Asia, politics is never enough—you must always back up your position with money. But were it to be acknowledged that Ching Wei traffics in heroin as well as opium, the American government would bring enormous pressure to bear against the Thai and Burmese governments. What hypocrites you Americans are! It is a well-known fact that your own CIA has engaged in the trafficking of opium as well as heroin here for many years." He paused for me to confirm or deny it, but I said nothing.

"Besides, as you well know, Ching Wei regards himself as a distinguished Chinese gentleman, and Chinese gentlemen do not dirty their hands in commerce, especially illegal commerce. Dirty hands mean dirty face. So he maintains the fiction that he is a Shan freedom fighter who merely taxes the evil opium dealers who pass his way. Of course, it is a sham, but to the Chinese, appearances are everything."

"But why is China White so important to Ching Wei? Is it really so different from the ordinary stuff?"

Hoffmann arched his bushy white brows at me as he paced around the lab. "As you know, China White makes ordinary heroin seem as mild as aspirin, just as heroin made morphine obsolete when it was first discovered years ago. Anyone who has been using China White for as long as Ching Wei can never be satisfied again with anything else. And only China White has succeeded in controlling the acute pain he suffers from that piece of shrapnel lodged in his liver. Not only does it relieve the physical pain, it also diminishes the chronic anger and depression which such traumatic wounds to the liver always cause. According to ancient Chinese medical theories, the liver houses the two basic emotions of anger and depression. China White prevents these emotions from flaring up all the time by cooling the fire in his liver."

"Why not just have the shrapnel surgically removed?"

"Impossible! It is too deeply embedded. We have consulted the best surgeons in Asia, and none would touch it. Besides, Ching Wei believes in the Chinese theory that surgery destroys the subtle channels through which the vital energy of chi travels through the body, and he will therefore have nothing to do with it. Can you imagine him submitting to several hours of anesthesia, while two strangers cut open his liver? Never happen!"

"So he relies on China White to relieve the pain and elevate his moods." Hoffmann nodded. "And cocaine to balance the negative side effects of China White." Another affirmative nod. "And since only Red China produces China White, he has to perform occasional favors for them to obtain it. And that's why he's got you working on the formula—to get the Chinese monkey off his back."

"Precisely!" Hoffmann's gray eyes beamed. With his bushy brows and tufts of snow-white hair, his drooping mustache and bony face, he looked like the mad scientist in a science fiction movie.

"Think you'll ever figure it out?"

But Hoffmann had already drifted off in thought, his brows furrowed. Suddenly, he snapped out of it, pulled a pack of Dunhills from a drawer, offered me one, and lit them with a Bunsen burner. "Jack, I have decided to confide everything to you. That is really why I invited you here this evening."

"I don't get it."

"I trust you. I also need you. And if you ever wish to regain your freedom, you need me too."

"I still don't get it." But it was beginning to sound interesting.

"You are the only person here who can fly that airplane. And that airplane is the only way to freedom from this place. The ticket to that freedom is the formula for China White." He looked around instinctively to see if anyone were eavesdropping as he unraveled his scheme.

"After all these years of research, I have discovered the preliminary stages for the production of China White. All that eludes me now is the final refinement process." He shrugged and blew a cloud of smoke at me. "Of course, I may never find it, but with a little luck and a lot of hard work, I predict that I will complete the formula within two years." He knocked on a wooden table for good luck.

"Then what?"

"Last year, Ching Wei obtained a fresh supply of his favorite 'Snowflake' brand of China White from the Chinese—enough to last him about three years at his current rate of consumption. Hopefully, I will have the formula ready shortly before his supply is exhausted. Then I will demand one million dollars in cash in exchange for the formula, plus your freedom to fly me and my family to Bangkok. From there I will return to Switzerland, where I can live what remains of my life in peace and quiet with my family."

"You've got plenty of peace and quiet here."

"Ach, it is not the same! I am an old man now, Jack, almost seventy. Old men, like young children, always long for home. I have had enough adventures in foreign lands, and I do not wish to grow old and die among strangers here in the jungle, so far from home . . ." Hoffmann's eyes glazed over as he fantasized his retirement.

The plan sounded insane to me. That formula was obviously worth more to Ching Wei than Hoffmann, me, and all the members of his menagerie rolled into one, and a million bucks was a mere drop in the bucket to him, but Hoffmann's plan did not account for Ching Wei's fanatical attachment to face and other traditional Chinese considerations, such as loyalty.

"I think you're crazy to even dream of doing such a thing," I told Hoffmann. "You know perfectly well how Ching Wei is about these things. After bankrolling your research all these years and treating you like a trusted ally, if you tried to squeeze him for money with the formula, he'd accuse you of treason and have you torn limb from limb and fed to the dogs, if not worse. Besides that, he'd never let you leave here until you give him the complete formula, and if you give him that, he'd never let you leave—at least not in one piece."

Hoffmann snapped out of it and focused his mind again. "For the formula he would do anything," he said confidently, "even swallow his pride. And my plan includes many precautions. After informing Ching Wei of my demands, I will . . ."

"Hold your horses, Hoffmann, I don't want to hear another word of it! The less you tell me, the less I know, and the less I know, the better. If you ever figure out the formula, and if you're crazy enough to try to pull this off, and by some miracle of nature Ching Wei actually agrees, then I'll fly you and your loot out of here, but only on the strict condition that you make it perfectly clear to him that this whole scheme is your idea, not mine. I don't ever want him to know that you told me a word about this in advance, because if it backfires on you, I don't want to get myself 'One Man, Two-Halved' or 'Red Butterflied' for being suspected as an accomplice. Are we in agreement on that?"

"Agreed!" He sucked on his cigarette and cocked an eyebrow at me. "So then, are you interested or not?"

"Let me sleep on it for a year or two, while you work on the formula. Meanwhile, your secret is safe with me. I'm no tattletale."

"'Tattletale'? That has a rather poetic ring to it. What does it mean? You must teach me more of these interesting American idioms."

I had just begun another lesson in American slang, when our conversation was interrupted by someone knocking on the door. A melodious voice trilled that dinner was ready.

"Coming, Liebling!" Hoffmann yelled, putting a finger to his lips to indicate our secret complicity. "Come now, Jack, let us enjoy the monkey stew and other delicacies Lulu has prepared for us. Like all good Chinese women, she is a wonderful cook. We will continue our discussion some other time."

XV

I was playing poker with a few guys at the bar in Poong late one night, when a stranger approached our table and sat down, uninvited. "Cut me in," he demanded.

The others all seemed to recognize him, and no one raised an eyebrow at his rude intrusion. Nor did anyone bother to introduce me, so I did it myself. "Jack Robertson," I extended a hand, "chief pilot, Dragon Mountain Airways."

"So you're the new flyboy, eh?" he drawled, ignoring my hand. He stuffed a chew of betel into his mouth and said, "Name's Lopper. Your deal, flyboy."

I dealt a five-card stud, and he drew an ace on the first card up. He bet big without looking at the card in the hole. "Where'd the Chink pick you up?" he asked.

"Northern Laos. I was flying a routine mission for Air America out of Saigon when this goon with one eye pops out of the cargo bay like a jack-in-the-box and hijacks my plane." I drew a jack on my third card, which paired up nicely with the one I had in the hole. I bet the pot and he raised me double. The rest of the table folded, and I dealt out the last card.

Lopper drew a queen and calmly bet the limit. I was sure he had another queen or an ace in the hole, which would have beat my pair of jacks, but my last card turned up a deuce, giving me a pair of twos showing, backed by a hidden pair of jacks. I saw his bet, and he turned up a pair of queens, but it wasn't good enough to beat my twin jacks and double deuces.

"Pretty slick," Lopper said, tossing in his cards. "Guy named Jack gets hijacked by a jack-in-the-box and holds a pair of jacks behind double deuce." He spat a puddle of betel juice onto the floor and barked, "Deal!" He played carelessly all night, but his luck ran well, and he ended up breaking even. The game folded up a little past midnight.

"Split a bottle, flyboy?" he suggested. We moved over to the bar, and he ordered a bottle of Jack Daniels. That's when I noticed the pistol tucked in his belt and the knife strapped to his calf. I knew that the only white men allowed to carry weapons in Ching Wei's domain were the Lurps.

Despite his gruff demeanor, Lopper had a bright mind and a good sense of humor. He looked about twenty-five years old and said he came from Tennessee. He'd been in Vietnam eighteen months when his squad was captured in Laos, and he viewed the whole war as a sick joke. When I told him that I'd met Ching Wei in Chungking back in '43 and had him busted for smuggling opium, Lopper whistled in amazement. He was fascinated by my stories about flying supplies over the Hump between India and China, and he demanded all kinds of technical details, right down to the type of weaponry we used then. "Man, that was a *real* war," he said, "a war with meaning and purpose, not a half-assed panty raid like Nam."

We drank till nearly dawn and both got stinking drunk, polishing off a bottle and a half of whiskey along with half a case of beer. He gave a hilarious account of how his squad had held off Ching Wei's Chinese troops in Laos. "No wonder those clowns lost China. Soon's the shit hits the fan, they squawk and scatter like a flock of frightened chickens, every man for himself."

When he finally fell off his barstool, we decided it was time to turn in. "Hey, man, you're all right," he slurred, draping a limp arm over my shoulder. "You're no chump like most of the turds around here. Ya gotta come up to our village some time and meet the rest of the guys."

"Great, I'll be there!" I'd been fishing for an invitation to visit his camp all evening. "When and where?"

Lopper got a pencil and paper from the barman and scrawled a rough map. "Head out towards the village where they hold those soccer games, but cut up the trail to the right at this checkpoint." He stabbed the paper with the pencil, tearing a jagged hole. "Follow the trail along the ridge about two miles till you come to a bamboo bridge. Cross the bridge over the ravine and keep following the trail till you get to our village. You'll know it when you get there," he laughed. "But lissen, pal, ya gotta tell me what day you wanna come so I can warn the boys not to blow your head off when you show up."

"How about Friday? Gotta make supply runs for Ching Wei on Wednesday and Thursday, but Friday I'm free."

"All right, man, Friday it is!" We toasted Friday with a last round of whiskey, then he lurched down the hallway in back of the bar, where the barman had prepared him a bunk. I grabbed my gear and stumbled back to Moreau's.

Bright and early Friday morning, I headed up into the hills. It was hot and humid, and by the time I reached the bamboo bridge, I was pouring sweat. The Lurp village was located about six miles north of Poong in a tangled, inaccessible corner of Ching Wei's kingdom. Across the bamboo bridge the trail abruptly grew narrow and overgrown, winding sharply uphill through huge trees and thick stands of bamboo. There wasn't a ten-yard stretch of trail that was straight, and about every fifty yards the path zigzagged through a dense maze of thorn hedge, deliberately planted there to discourage uninvited visitors. The thorns were sharp as needles and tough as steel. I shuddered at the thought of attempting to negotiate that trail by night.

I'd just passed safely through the third maze, when two men suddenly stepped out from the trees and silently trained their rifles on me—Karen, judging by their tattoos, not Shan. They scrutinized me for a minute, then lowered their guns and melted back into the forest. Apparently Lopper had told them who to look for that morning.

Beyond the last maze the trail became straight and wide open again, and in the distance I saw a few signs of human habitation. Thatched huts on stilts stood snugly against the side of a steep mountain. Smoke from cooking fires wove a haze over the village, and there were women and children roaming around. Along the final approach to the village, two rows of huge mountain oak, as neat and evenly spaced as in a city park, stood sentry. All other vegetation had been cleared from the trail.

The moment I entered that shady lane, my spine turned to ice and I froze in my tracks. Each tree had a little shelf neatly carved into its trunk at eye level, and from each shelf a severed human head stared balefully at all passersby. Though a bit weathered, the heads were intact and well preserved, blank eyes wide open, skin tanned like leather, tufts of hair trembling in the breeze. I counted twenty-four heads as I strode by, twelve on each side of the path. Most of them were Chinese or local, with a few whites scattered among them. The fresher ones looked remarkably alive, and though some of the older ones were getting a bit gray and mottled, none had decayed or been attacked by bugs. Chills ran up and down my spine, and I quickened my pace to get past that silent host.

Waiting for me at the top of the path stood Lopper. Instead of the combat fatigues he'd worn on his visit to Poong, he was dressed in a bright yellow sarong and straw sandals. He greeted me with a slap on the back and a big laugh. "Now you know why they call me 'Lopper!' The Wild Wa do it up north. Keeps evil spirits out of their villages, and reminds unwanted visitors where they'll end up if they go any farther."

As we strolled through the village, he told me how he'd picked up his hobby. "Ching Wei sent us up north to the Kachen Hills. Too many Bur-Coms there, getting much too close for comfort. Good soldiers when they have to be, so Ching Wei sent us up to take a look.

"Late one afternoon, we pitched camp in a deep ravine, and

one of our guys stepped into the woods to take a crap. He never came back. We found his body slumped over his own shit, with a poison dart in his back and his head missing."

Lopper had sent a scout back to fetch up twenty Karen hunters, and they tracked down the Wa village responsible for the beheading. "We staked it out and went in at the crack of dawn one morning, using tiger shit to spook their watchdogs. Old Chinese trick, and nothing does the job better. The moment any dog gets a whiff of tiger shit, he runs for the nearest shelter and hides there, silent as stone. Pure instinct; never fails. We got the shit from Ching Wei's zoo."

They caught the village sound asleep and torched the huts, mowing down everyone in sight as they ran out in panic. "The place was filthy, and so were the people. We finally found the village sawbwa hiding in a woodpile and demanded that he return our buddy's head. He took us over to a hovel on the edge of the village, where the old man who preserved heads lived. The stench was incredible! I almost greased the old bastard on the spot, but then I had a better idea. I lopped off the sawbwa's head right in front of the old man and ordered him to preserve it for me. At first he stalled, so I poked out one of his eyes. That did the trick. We took a few more heads for souvenirs, and brought them and the old man back here to show us how to preserve them. It's a long, complicated process handed down from father to son and known only to the Wild Wa. The old buzzard also showed us how to cut the shelves into the trees without killing them. That's how I started my collection."

Their village was small and tidy, not cluttered and sprawling like the others. About two dozen huts were snugly built against the slope of the mountain, supported on sturdy stilts. I saw no field or paddy under cultivation there, not even a vegetable patch, so I asked Lopper what they did for food.

"We don't have to worry about that shit," he replied. "The Chink gave us two villages down the valley to support and supply us. Every morning they deliver fresh meat and vegetables, fruit and rice, betel and opium—whatever we want. And they provide building materials and labor whenever we need some new construction done around here. No one else lives in our village except us and our women and kids." He kicked his sandals off at the foot of a bamboo ladder and started climbing up. "This here's my place." I stepped out of my shoes and followed him up.

"Hiya, Lopper!" a voice squawked as we appeared on the polished hardwood planks of an open terrace up above. The voice belonged to a big green and red parrot that preened and strutted at the sight of its master. Though the place looked like an ordinary native hut from the outside, it was as nicely furnished inside as Dr. Hoffmann's house. Lopper said that the native style of housing was the most practical and comfortable in that climate, but he saw no reason to live like a peasant on the inside.

We sat on rattan chairs out on the veranda, which commanded a fine view of the village and the valleys beyond. "Only thing we ain't got up here is electricity," Lopper remarked, "and who needs that when you got people to do all the work for you?"

A gorgeous Shan girl came out onto the veranda, dressed in nothing but a flimsy sarong slung low on her hips. She couldn't have been a day over eighteen. Lopper rattled at her in the local lingo, and off she went to fetch refreshments. She returned with a bottle of red wine and two crystal glasses, some fresh fruit and dried meat, and a lacquered box that looked like a humidor.

Lopper poured us some wine and flipped open the lid of the box, pointing with pride at its contents. "This here's the best goddamn ganja in Burma! Grow it myself from Thai seed. Good weed beats opium any day—much more stony—and you don't get hooked on it." He rolled a fat marijuana cigarette thick as a cigar—he called it a "spliff"— using some kind of dried tree leaf as a wrapper, and we smoked in silence for a while. An automatic weapon burped sporadically in the background, vaguely reminding me of Hsu's New Year raid.

"Relax, man. That's just Katz, shooting up another case of ammo. Target practice. He goes through a couple of cases a month keeping his shooting eye sharp. Long-range sniper shots, fast-draw from the hip, automatic weapons, handguns, shotguns—you name it—Katz is the best damn shot in the kingdom.

Ching Wei likes nothing better than a good shot, so he gives Katz all the ammo he needs to keep in shape."

"How many guys you got living up here now?"

"Ten. Had an even dozen when we started out from Nam, but one guy bought it in that firefight with the Chink's troops; then Simpson went and lost his head to the Wild Wa up north. Just us ten little soldiers now . . ."

The more Lopper smoked, the more he rambled, but eventually the whole story came out. After fighting off Ching Wei's men for two days and killing half of them, the Lurps had run out of ammo and had to surrender. They were dragged bound and gagged back to Dragon Mountain and thrown into cages like a bunch of wild animals. Still they managed to kill two guards with their bare hands while being fed. This only impressed Ching Wei more, and he refused to punish them.

"One day a bunch of guards came down to get us and said that we'd been invited out to dinner," Lopper recounted, snorting with laughter. "Dragged us up to the palace in chains and brought us to this big bathhouse somewhere in the gardens. There they stripped us naked—boy, did we stink—and threw us inside, posting armed guards at the door and windows. Waiting for us inside were a dozen of Ching Wei's most beautiful maids, all stark naked. They washed us, shaved us, massaged us, blew us, and did all kinds of other nice things to us. Amazing what a woman can do for a man! Couple of hours later, we came out of there smelling like roses and dressed in long Chinese robes. There was a huge banquet waiting for us inside the palace, and after we finished stuffing ourselves, Ching Wei himself came in and introduced himself."

Lopper sent a big blue smoke ring sailing up toward his parrot, which ruffled its feathers and squawked in protest. "He kept us there for two weeks, treating us like kings and talking with us like old buddies. Well, eventually he made us an offer we couldn't refuse. He told us we could stay together as a unit instead of being scattered all over the kingdom like the rest of his so-called guests. He gave us this whole mountain for ourselves and had this village specially built for us. He gave us two more villages down the valley for logistical support and daily supplies, and he told us we could keep the Shan maids who serviced us the first day. I still remember his final words after making his offer: "Why live like peasants in America when you may live like kings here in Burma?"

"And what's your end of the deal?"

"He just wanted two things from us. One, to serve as his reconnaissance patrol and security team. Two, to take a solemn pledge of allegiance to him. Chinks put a lot of stock in formalities like that—gives them 'big face' or something. The pledge was an elaborate affair that took all day and ended with another big party in the palace. As for the work, there's a little recon now and then, occasional sabotage and assassination missions, and, of course, hunting down escapers and deserters. It's all the same to us, except now we work for him instead of Uncle Sam. Compared to him, Uncle Sam's a cheapskate, and compared to here, America's like a prison." He laughed and flipped the ganja butt over the rail. "We haven't blown a mission yet, and every time we wrap one up, he heaps more gifts and honors on us. I tell you, Jack, it sure beats pumping gas in Detroit!"

Lopper took me around the village and introduced me to some of the other Lurps. They all lived like princes in cozy homes similar to Lopper's. There was Katz, still shooting up a storm at a target range on the edge of the village and a guy called Hunch, an enormous Texan who preferred fighting with knives, crossbows, hatchets, blowguns, bare hands—anything but firearms. Hunch once volunteered to put on a show for one of Ching Wei's parties. With a fish knife in one hand and a Wa war club in the other, he took on six of Ching Wei's Bur-Com prisoners, all of them armed with the same weapons. It was no contest: Hunch had them bludgeoned to a bloody pulp and gutted in less than fifteen minutes.

Weasel was a wiry little guy from Manhattan who worked best alone and at night. Often he'd take a couple of Karen scouts and disappear for weeks at a time into Laos. He'd heard rumors of POW camps there, where American GIs were still being held from the Vietnam War, and he was determined to find them. "We gotta get them outta there before they're traded off in some dirty deal and sent back to the States. Those guys'll never make it back in America after what they've been through. I'm gonna find them and bring them back here." Weasel used no drugs whatsoever and spent several hours each day keeping himself in fighting form.

They even had a philosophical Yale graduate among them, a guy they called Teach. Teach liked to lecture the rest of the group on the ethical and cosmic implications of their various missions, and he was a highly trained demolitions technician. The other four were out on patrol, and I didn't meet them until a few weeks later.

We returned to Lopper's veranda for more wine and another smoke. "The other four are out scouting the terrain for our next mission—the biggest one yet," Lopper explained. "And I didn't invite you up here today just to sit around smoking dope and bullshitting all afternoon."

"What, then?"

"Business."

"What kind of business?"

"Revenge business, sweet and simple."

"I'm listening."

"That asshole Colonel Hsu really fucked things up around here with his little Tet offensive. Ching Wei lost about fifty of his best troops. Poong was raped and burned to the ground, and you—you lost a fine woman and a great family." My blood boiled at the memory of that loss.

"The Chink wants us to deal with this jerk and finish him off once and for all. He's put up with his bullshit long enough. It's a tough mission, but we figure we can pull it off real nice and easy, *if* you join the game."

"Me?"

"Yup, you. Hsu's camp is well fortified, and he's got plenty of men to defend it. What we need in order to nab him are the elements of speed and surprise. From the air, Hsu's a sitting duck. So he won't be expecting the surprise we have in store for him. The plan calls for you and me to fly high over his camp with special air-recon cameras and take a few shots of the area so that we know the layout. When the time comes, we'll fly that crate of yours in low and soften up the camp with cluster bombs and incendiaries, while the rest of the boys take advantage of the chaos to rush in and take Hsu out of there. You see, Ching Wei insists we bring him back alive so that he can enjoy the pleasure of killing him his own way."

"And Ching Wei suggested I help you out?"

"Nope, that was my idea. The night I met you at the bar in Poong, I'd just come down from the palace with the Chink's final okay for our game plan. But instead of assigning you to the mission himself, he insists that *we* get you to volunteer. That makes *us* responsible if you try anything funny, like escape. Get it?"

"Got it."

He detailed the entire plan for me, then looked me straight in the eye and asked, "Interested?"

"You can bet on it. Deal me in!" I couldn't resist the excitement of a combat mission after years of being a delivery boy, and my heart thumped at the prospect of avenging the deaths of Suraya and her family.

"That's what I figured," Lopper said, flashing me one of his rare smiles. "Reason I drank and played poker with you that night in Poong was to check you out, to see how you play your cards and how you hold your booze. Hell, I *know* you're good at your job, but you can't *trust* a man until you've drunk and gambled with him."

The Shan girl appeared on the veranda again and set lunch out on the table. Like me, Lopper had adopted the local diet and local eating habits, so we rinsed our mouths and washed our fingers in a basin of water, then tucked into the curries, rice, and condiments with our bare hands. After lunch, the girl cleared the table and brought us coffee and fresh fruit.

"Lopper wanna whopper!" the parrot screeched, right on cue, reminding his master that it was time for his after-lunch smoke. Lopper gave the bird a biscuit and rolled another big spliff of ganja.

As Lopper got higher, the sun sank lower, and suddenly I remembered the gauntlet of thorn mazes I had to pass through in order to get back to Poong. "Better get my ass back down the trail before it gets too dark to see."

"Damn right," he agreed. "Even we steer clear of that trail at night—except for Weasel, who sails through those thorns like Br'er Rabbit."

We climbed back down the ladder, and he escorted me to the top of the trail. "Good to get to know you, Jack," he said, pumping my hand. "We'll deal you in on the Hsu mission and work out a schedule soon. See you in a couple of weeks."

I'd forgotten about the silent sentries who kept vigil over the approach to the village from their niches in the oaks. In the fast-fading light, they looked strangely expressive and malevolent, reminding all who passed how miserable it is to be dead, and how good to be alive.

XVI

To supplement his own opium harvests, Ching Wei bought large quantities of the stuff from the Bur-Com insurgents, whose 20,000 well-armed troops controlled most of the Kachen highlands in northeastern Burma.

Originally, the Burmese Communist movement refused to deal in opium as a matter of principle, just like the Chinese Nationalists when they crossed into Burma from China thirty years ago. But in order to curry political favor with Rangoon, Peking abruptly terminated all financial and material aid to the Bur-Com group in 1975, leaving them to fend for themselves. To survive and keep their movement alive, they started collecting opium grown in areas under their control and selling it to Ching Wei, Colonel Hsu, and other Chinese dealers in the region.

Ironic, isn't it? When Ching Wei, Colonel Hsu, and other Chinese Nationalist officers first came to Burma in 1949, all they wanted to do was fight the Communists and recover China. Only when Taipei cut them off in 1958 did they resort to the opium trade for survival. Same story with the Bur-Coms. When they started out, generously backed by Peking, all they wanted to do was fight capitalism and overthrow the government in Rangoon. Then Peking cut them off, and they too went into the opium business. Finally, we show up to prevent Communist North Vietnam from taking over the entire region, but then Washington suddenly does an about-face and cuts us off too, refusing to even acknowledge our operations out here. So we also go into the opium business to finance our activities. Now everyone here is involved in the opium trade, and no one gives a hoot about the politics that brought us all out here in the first place. Small wonder guys like Thompson profiteered so much on the side—almost seems like Company policy. Only wish I'd done more of it myself while I had the chance.

Instead, I was now an errand boy for the biggest profiteer of them all. Not only did I fly Ching Wei's opium to Thailand, I also brought back all the luxuries for his palace: Scotch whiskey, French cognac, American cigarettes, Cuban cigars, movies and magazines, guns and ammo—you name it, I flew it in. I even flew cartons of Kotex back to Dragon Mountain for his women.

Meanwhile, Ching Wei and Lopper plotted revenge against Colonel Hsu. Prior to the New Year massacre, Ching Wei had tolerated Hsu's continuing operations in the region because it worked to his own advantage. Hsu himself had once been the kingpin of the drug trade in the Golden Triangle, and as far as government authorities were concerned, he still was. That took the heat off Ching Wei, who preferred to keep a low public profile. But Hsu's last desperate attempt to regain his former position by attacking Ching Wei at home was a big mistake, for it broke Ching Wei's patience. Worse yet, the attack had come at Chinese New Year, an unforgivable breach of Chinese etiquette and a direct slap in Ching Wei's face. Only unequivocal revenge could redress this insult.

Colonel Hsu's camp straddled the border between Burma and Thailand about a hundred miles south of Dragon Mountain. Ever since Ching Wei had deposed him, Hsu's operations had been reduced to a petty protection racket. He and his ragtag band wandered the opium trails in and around the Golden Triangle, plundering the weakest caravans, extorting money from others, and steering clear of major dealers with big armies. Once a proud and powerful warlord, Hsu was now a hit-and-run sneak thief, and he laid the blame for his disgrace squarely on Ching Wei's shoulders.

"That bastard offspring of a barnyard sow will soon have cause to regret his rash behavior at New Year," Ching Wei vowed at one of his summer parties. He always spoke Chinese when cussing people out. English curses sound mild by comparison. "That mongrel should 'piss a puddle and have a look at himself in it.'" He also loved to pepper his speech with the sayings of Confucius and other ancient Chinese sages. "Clearly he has 'failed to take the proper measure of himself,'" he accused, "and for that 'he will taste the bitter fruits of the evil seeds he has sown.'"

As usual, Lopper's plan relied entirely on the elements of speed and surprise, executed with perfect timing and teamwork. During the first stage, I flew over Hsu's camp while Lopper and a Chinese technician photographed the terrain with special aerial reconnaissance equipment Ching Wei had obtained for the purpose. Hsu was holed up in a remote ravine deep in the mountains, and overland reconnaissance would have been impossible without being detected. Lopper's equipment permitted us to photograph the lay of the land from an altitude of over ten thousand feet—too high to draw small-arms fire, or even be noticed from the ground.

With typical Chinese patience, Ching Wei waited almost a full year before executing his plan. By that time we had thoroughly mapped out Hsu's camp, including all possible avenues of access and escape. When the time was ripe, Ching Wei cleverly took advantage of Hsu's incorrigible greed to launch the plan. He sent a small caravan of opium on two dozen ponies, escorted by only fifty Shan tribesmen armed with old carbines, directly south, where Hsu's scouts were bound to pick up the scent. Sure enough they did, and Hsu immediately dispatched 300 men to ambush it. The Shan escort was privy to the plan and put up only token resistance before scattering like chickens into the hills, leaving the ponies and cargo behind. Prize in hand, Hsu's raiding party proudly marched the booty right back into Hsu's camp, exactly as Ching Wei planned it.

But it was the proverbial Trojan Horse. The bundles on the ponies' backs contained no opium. Instead, they were tightly packed with 2,000 pounds of plastic explosive bundled together with sharp shrapnel and nails. Lopper and I observed the scene through a powerful lens from the plane, 5,000 feet overhead. As the caravan pulled into camp, with Hsu's men still marching beside it and throngs of others milling around to greet them, Lopper let out a loud war whoop and detonated the caravan by remote control. Most of the men were killed in the initial burst of fire and steel. Then I dived in low and swooped over the camp, while Lopper dropped a hail of cluster bombs and incendiaries from the cargo bay. Our part of the job was done in less than ten minutes.

Down below, Katz and the rest of the Lurps, backed by 250 of Ching Wei's best Chinese troops and Shan scouts, lay in wait. When the camp was in flames, they moved in quickly and took it by storm, meeting only token resistance from the confused survivors. Katz had Hsu's private living quarters surrounded within minutes of entering the camp and literally caught him with his pants down. He'd been soaking in a hot bath with his favorite concubine when the caravan entered his camp and exploded. But the raid was so swift and sudden that before Hsu even had a chance to dry off and get dressed, Katz had him in hand. They made him march back to Dragon Mountain barefoot and naked.

I attended Hsu's last supper along with others who'd lost friends and family in the New Year massacre. Typically, Ching Wei decided to immerse Hsu in life's sweetest pleasures before sending him to a terrifying death. The lovely concubine who'd been caught in the tub with him was brought along to share his last night of life. Ching Wei's women had dressed and coiffed her to female perfection, and she looked beautiful.

When I arrived, Ching Wei and his guests were already sipping cocktails in the throne room. Hoffmann and Wellington were there, and so was Jim Thompson. Colonel Hsu sat by himself in an armchair, glumly sipping cognac and staring at the carpet. Like the rest of us, he wore a long silk robe cut in classical

Chinese style, except his was white, the traditional color of mourning in China. That was typical of Ching Wei's style: he had invited Hsu to his own wake, to mourn his own death, while the rest of us celebrated.

I grabbed a Scotch and approached Hoffmann. "Kind of perverse, isn't it, all this Last Supper crap? Can't imagine Hsu having much of an appetite tonight."

"Perverse?" Hoffmann intoned, rolling the r's in his thick German accent. "Not at all! This banquet is not for Hsu, but for those like you who lost loved ones in the attack."

"Oh, yeah? How about Todd Wellington over there? He's a bachelor. Who'd he lose?"

"Ah!" Hoffmann lowered his voice and wagged his bushy brows. "It was Todd, in fact, who insisted on personally packing the explosives that blew up Hsu's camp. You see, he lost Bondi, his steady companion and bedmate for the past five years. Bondi was his, ah, 'little rabbit,' as the Chinese say—his catamite, his joy-boy." Hoffmann hunched up his shoulders and rocked on his heels with laughter at my surprise. "Like you, Todd was well treated here from the very beginning, due to his special training as an engineer. He was lodged in Poong with a wealthy family that had four charming daughters and two young sons. Imagine the family's frustration when, night after night, each daughter in turn reported failure in arousing Todd's amorous interests. They tried everything, for Todd is one of Ching Wei's most important assistants, and the family had much to gain by providing him a wife. Then imagine, if you can, their even greater surprise when one afternoon they discovered Todd fellating their youngest son, a comely boy of only fourteen, out in a bamboo grove behind their house. Apparently, the boy enjoyed it as much as Todd, and so, with characteristic Oriental resignation, they gave Todd a son instead of a daughter. This greatly amused Ching Wei, and he permitted the relationship. He built them a small cottage in Poong, and they were treated like any other married couple. There they lived together very happily until one of Hsu's men threw a grenade into their hut that night and blew his beloved Bondi to pieces. The only thing that has prevented

Todd from going insane with grief has been the promise of revenge."

"Good Lord, poor bastard!"

"Ah, Captain Jack," Ching Wei's voice interrupted as he approached from behind. "Come, I want you to meet our guest of honor." He switched to formal Mandarin and introduced me to Hsu. *"Colonel Hsu, this is my chief pilot, Captain Luo Bao-shan, whose family you murdered last year. He has been very helpful in bringing you here tonight."*

Wearily, Hsu raised his gray, crew-cut head and stared at me with eyes devoid of feeling. He knew he was a dead man, and he was trying to maintain composure.

The banquet began promptly at 7:30, and, as usual, Ching Wei's kitchen outdid itself providing the best Chinese food this side of Shanghai. Among the girls assigned to serve our table stood Hsu's kidnapped concubine, fighting bravely to hold back the tears that kept flooding her eyes.

Despite the occasion—or perhaps because of it—the food tasted better than ever. Ching Wei had carefully instructed his chefs to prepare the most succulent gourmet delicacies from Hsu's native province of Canton, flavors which Hsu had not tasted since leaving China over thirty years ago. The familiar fragrance and flavors of home evoked such strong visceral memories of his life and family back in China that with every bite of food his resistance to Ching Wei's hospitality melted, until finally he too was tucking into the dishes with gusto. Ching Wei was determined to destroy Hsu's resolve to die bravely, and food was his first weapon.

The shark fin stew with Yunnan ham almost brought tears of joy to the doomed man's eyes. The aroma of an approaching platter of freshwater crabs steamed in wine and ginger made him jerk his head around with involuntary anticipation. The dish that finally broke him down entirely was a huge Mandarin fish braised with "Five Precious Flavors," a legendary gourmet delight long favored by Chinese emperors. After that, Hsu forgot about his fate and indulged wholeheartedly in the endless array of food and wine, just as Ching Wei intended.

During dinner, Hoffmann quietly informed me that Hsu's wine had been spiked with a potent blend of Chinese herbal aphrodisiacs and testosterone, a blend developed by Hoffmann himself. "Ching Wei uses it sometimes. It is guaranteed to render Colonel Hsu incapable of resisting the pleasures of his concubine's flesh later tonight." He would lie in her arms all night, Hoffmann said, horny as a rabbit, hot as a piston, unable and unwilling to prepare himself mentally and emotionally for the ordeal he faced the following day.

By the end of the banquet, Hsu was indeed quite drunk, sated with good food, and burning with desire for his woman. He laughed hilariously at the Chinese jokes Ching Wei kept throwing his way, and he even babbled in broken English with some of the other guests.

At precisely noon the next day, Hsu's party was over. The guards dragged him naked and kicking, still hot and sticky with lust, from the arms of his concubine and paraded him around the village in a dunce cap. He'd had no time to deal with his fear and properly prepare himself for death, so he made a hell of a fuss, completely losing his dignity, just as Ching Wei intended. Before taking his life, Ching Wei had decided to strip him of his face, the ultimate Chinese insult.

There must have been two thousand people jammed into the village square to witness the execution. A row of chairs was set up front for Ching Wei, Todd, Hoffmann, Thompson, myself, and a few others who'd attended the banquet the night before. Ching Wei's Black Dragons held Hsu firmly in hand at the edge of a man-sized pit dug into the ground.

When Ching Wei gave the signal, the guards lowered Hsu into the hole and buried him up to his ribcage. He screamed and flailed his arms, apparently aware now of exactly what Ching Wei had in store for him. Ching Wei studied him for a few minutes in silence, then clapped his hands for the execution to begin. As usual, it had a flowery Chinese name, which completely belied the gruesome nature of the punishment. Roughly translated, it means something innocuous like "Pop Goes the Weasel."

While one guard held Hsu's head firmly in place, another inscribed a cross on top of his skull with a razor. Peeling back the four flaps of skin left by the incision, they gradually separated his scalp from his skull, until the top of his head lay entirely exposed. The crowd stared on in complete silence, and the only sound to be heard was Hsu's terrified screaming. Two guards carefully stretched open the flaps of skin like a laundry bag, while another slowly poured a heavy fluid into the opening from a large jug. It was pure liquid mercury. Whenever the cavity brimmed up with mercury, the guard stopped pouring long enough for it to work its way down between skin and flesh, thereby slowly separating the two tissues as it sunk deeper and deeper inside. They continued this process for about half an hour.

Gravity gradually drew the heavy mercury down through the soft subcutaneous tissues. Each time the level dropped a bit, the guard poured a little more in through his open scalp, and the additional weight caused increasingly greater downward pressure beneath the skin. Pretty soon his head, chest, shoulders, and arms were bloated up like ripe melons. He looked like a balloon about to burst.

Finally, the mercury began to inch its way down into the portions of his body buried beneath the ground. The deeper it sank, the more the guards poured in, creating irresistible pressure between skin and flesh. When the weight of the mercury beneath his skin exceeded the weight of his own flesh and bones, the weasel suddenly popped. All at once, the mercury forced its way down into his legs with a rending rush, displacing his body in the hole. He popped out of his skin like a ripe banana squeezed in a fist, and a gasp rippled through the crowd. There he stood, pink and slimy as a freshly skinned rabbit, a mass of raw muscles twitching grotesquely in the noonday sun.

Even the guards winced at the sight, and they steered clear of his staggering steps. Chills ran up and down my spine, and I felt the gorge rising in my throat. Todd, despite his initial vengeance, vomited violently in his own lap, but he held his place. Ching Wei just sat there calmly, lit a cigarette, and gazed at the gore with interest as he smoked. A pool of mercury shimmered in the hole where Hsu had been buried moments earlier, and his skin lay in a rumpled heap around the rim, like a discarded bathrobe.

Flies were buzzing over Hsu's convulsing body when Ching Wei finally dismissed us. We all left the scene immediately, except Ching Wei, who sat there and watched Hsu slowly die all afternoon.

XVII

"I know they're in there!" Weasel blurted to no one in particular. "I saw them!" He was sitting in a corner of Lopper's veranda, poring over a map of Laos. He looked up at Lopper, and shouted, "When we gonna go in and take them out, man?"

Lopper sighed. "Man, you are all work and no play! Relax, already!" Everyone, except Weasel, was very relaxed; stewed to the gills, in fact. The Lurps were throwing a party to celebrate the successful completion of the Hsu mission, and I was the only outsider invited. I liked those guys a lot by then, and the feeling seemed to be mutual. We were all sprawled around Lopper's terrace, smoking and drinking; except Weasel, who did neither.

"Look," Lopper said, "the Chink has already agreed to let us do it, even though there's nothing in it for him. That's our reward for nailing Hsu. We've got the green light now, so relax. We'll get around to it soon enough."

"Yeah," Katz chimed in, "relax! Have a hit of this here spliff." He handed Weasel one of Lopper's huge ganja cigars, but Weasel brushed it off. Katz was still basking in the glory of all the honors and gifts, including a brand-new bazooka, Ching Wei had heaped on him for leading the squad that snatched Hsu from his bathtub and marched him back to Dragon Mountain for execution. Now it was Weasel's turn to lead a mission into Laos, a mission he'd been hankering to launch for a long time.

Weasel had finally found what he'd been looking for in Laos: three POW camps where U.S. servicemen were still being held captive from the Vietnam War. He and his Karen scouts had come to within fifty yards of the fence line at one camp, where he counted at least thirty American inmates. He knew the location of two other camps, and he wanted to liberate them all, one by one. "Hell, man, we could use more guys like that around here," Weasel said. "Most of the ginks Ching Wei's men bring back here are totally useless—just a bunch of drunken derelicts."

"Need any help?" I offered.

"Thanks, but no thanks," Lopper cut in. "Aircraft can't be used on this one; gotta do it overland and go in at night. And that's risky for anyone who isn't well trained for it. Ching Wei'd never let you go on a mission like this. If you got killed, who'd fly that crate for him?"

I was quite drunk by then and tried to talk them into taking me along anyway, even without Ching Wei's permission, but by the next morning I'd completely forgotten about the whole thing. I'd passed out on Lopper's veranda and woken up with a splitting headache.

It was during that stoned afternoon at the Lurp village that I first got wind of the kid they called the "Prince of Laos." I'd seen him strolling through the village a few times before on previous visits—a handsome young boy elegantly dressed in the traditional silk attire of Lao royalty. He lived in splendid luxury in a fancy bungalow at the far end of the village, attended by his own team of servants, and everyone there, especially the locals, treated him with the utmost respect and affection. But whenever I asked Lopper about him, he just mumbled something about "an old friend of the family" and quickly changed the subject. That afternoon, however, thanks to all the booze and ganja, Lopper loosened up a bit and told me a little more about him.

"Brought him along with us from Laos when we first came here," Lopper slurred. "Great kid, nice guy. A son of the last king of Laos and one of his minor wives. When we told the Chink who he was and that we wanted to keep him here with us as our mascot, he said OK." Lopper paused to puff on the spliff Katz had passed him, and blew a cloud of smoke eastward in the direction of Laos. "One of these days," he said softly, "we're gonna take him back to Luang Prabang and put him on the throne where he belongs." Then he raised his glass and shouted out loud, "Long live the King!" We all drained our glasses, and that's the last thing I remember about it. The rest of the afternoon passed in a blur, and the subject never came up again after that. I never did find out how the Lurps met the boy, or why they brought him back to Dragon Mountain with them.

Two weeks later, Weasel led a strike squad of Lurps and Karen scouts, backed by a unit of Shan, into Laos and raided the camp where he'd spotted the prisoners. He was right; they were holding thirty-five American POWs there. The camp was located deep in northern Laos, near the border with North Vietnam, and Lopper later told me that he'd never seen such lax security. Some of the guards on duty were lying on a mat in the watchtower smoking opium, while others sat around a table at the main gate playing cards and drinking beer. The last thing the Pathet Lao expected up there was to be attacked from the rear by a band of Shan tribesmen led by half a dozen American commandos.

They went in at night, and Hunch killed the sentries with poison darts shot silently from a Wa blowgun. Teach blew up the barracks and supply depot, then they stormed the camp. Twenty minutes later, they were trotting back to Burma with twenty-nine bewildered POWs in tow; six got killed in the firefight.

Ching Wei welcomed the new arrivals to Poong with great pomp and ceremony. American flags festooned the village, and a loudspeaker blared the Star-Spangled Banner. A lot of those guys had been held in captivity for six or seven years, and they looked like walking ghosts. Ching Wei billeted them in guest bungalows within the palace grounds for a few weeks to fatten them up and calm them down. He also took the time to get to know them individually, for there was a lot of military talent among them, and Ching Wei intended to tap it.

I talked with a Navy flier named Reeves at a party in the palace a few weeks later. He'd been shot down over North Vietnam and held as a POW for over seven years.

"At first they kept us in a camp near Hanoi. But when we started bombing the north, they moved us out to Laos, so we wouldn't get killed in the air raids. I was shuttled between four different camps in Laos for five years, and all of them were holding American prisoners. Far's I know, they're still out there, rotting in the jungle. Reds kept telling us the war's still on and never going to end."

Reeves told me that their captors tried to make these guys give up hope and go native, and according to him, some of them have done just that. First they have to sign "confessions" that would get them shot for treason back home—or so the guards tell them. Then they're taken out and permitted to live in remote villages deep in the north, under constant surveillance. Eventually they marry local women and work as farmers or craftsmen. Those who refuse remain in prison camps forever. Sounds like a commie version of Dragon Mountain.

Of course, the POWs thought that Lopper and his crew were U.S. troops sent in to rescue them, and that Poong was just a base camp en route back home. They raised a hell of a stink when they found out the truth, but eventually they settled down and adjusted to the situation just like everyone else. At least they were better off at Dragon Mountain than in Laos. And I suspect Weasel was right when he said that they were a lot better off at Dragon Mountain than back in the States.

I had to hand it to Weasel. He'd done more for those guys than the entire U.S. government had done or ever would do. Hundreds of our servicemen still rotting away out there in filthy prison camps in the jungles of northern Laos, and the world just goes on. It's a crying shame we haven't done anything about that.

XVIII

With Hsu out of the way, Ching Wei had no more serious rivals to contend with in the region, and the next few years were relatively quiet. I spent a lot of time at home cultivating the "Long Life" exercises Old Lee had taught me back in Chungking, and gradually I recovered some of the subtle sensitivities to energy and spirit that had lain dormant within me for so long. By then I needed only four or five hours of sleep at night, and I could hike for miles in the hills without feeling winded.

My days usually began with a light breakfast out on Moreau's veranda: coffee, papaya, and *tupa*, which is a native dish consisting of rice flour, fresh coconut cream, and raw palm sugar steamed in a bamboo tube. You eat it by mashing a chunk of banana into the cooked tupa, then rolling it into a ball and popping it into your mouth. It's a delicious breakfast and a potent energy food.

After a shower and a shit, I'd wander down to the village to sit and smoke under my favorite bodhi tree, while waiting for the shop to open. Then I'd return to the house in time to have lunch with my daughter and Moreau's wife and help a bit with the housework. If no flights were scheduled that day, I'd spend the rest of the afternoon hiking in the mountains, tending the garden, or reading the latest magazines down at the bar in the village. Things could have been worse.

One sweltering summer afternoon, I was clearing a new patch of ground in the garden so that we could plant some lettuce seeds that Moreau had finally managed to obtain. The only things Moreau missed about France were fresh green garden salads and French cigarettes. At least now he'd have his salad.

It was so hot and humid that afternoon, that I wore nothing but a loincloth, my favorite piece of native clothing. Compared to loincloths, underpants feel like whalebone girdles. Suddenly, a familiar tingle tickled the back of my neck, ran down my spine, and landed in my gut with a shudder, an infallible signal that someone was intensely observing me. I spun around and found Moreau's wife Loma standing half-hidden behind a big banana leaf, her coal black eyes sparkling with mischief. The expression on her face, and the vibrations she generated, left no room for doubt about her intentions. Despite my effort to suppress it, a throbbing erection rose up in my loincloth.

She took that as a cue. Without a word, she stepped out from behind the foliage, tugged at a knot on her sarong, and let it drop to her feet. The sight of her smooth brown body naked in the lush green garden took my breath away. The last time I'd seen a naked woman was at one of Ching Wei's drunken orgies six months earlier. My resistance melted. I dropped the hoe, and we approached each other like magnets. As soon as we touched, she tore away my loincloth and pulled me down to the ground on top of her. From all the gnashing and thrashing, gouging and groaning that followed, I gathered that she'd gone without sex for at least as long as I had.

Loma had conveniently sent both our daughters down to the village to visit friends, and Moreau would not be home till dusk, so we went at it like rabbits all afternoon. She was wonderful—one of those shy, retiring, yet very dignified women, who explode with pent-up energy the moment you push the right buttons. Having carried a baby, her sexuality was fully developed and her appetite was boundless. Thanks to Old Lee's exercises, I was in perfect condition to keep up with her all afternoon.

Later, when I expressed concern that Moreau might come home early and catch me with my hand in his cookie jar, Loma laughed. She told me that Moreau had been impotent for almost three years due to his heavy opium smoking habit. Even his rare, half-hearted attempts to please her with what she called "French tongue-fucking" were few and far between. He'd simply lost all interest in sex. So she'd finally confronted him with her frustration and formally requested his permission to satisfy her needs with me. Like a true tribesman, Moreau had no objection to his wife sleeping with his good friend and honored guest. Matter of fact, he was delighted. He would now be completely free of the sexual duties he'd grown to loathe, and his wife could find her pleasure in the arms of someone he liked and trusted, rather than with some drunken lout down in the village. He gave us both his blessing and bought Loma an expensive bolt of Thai silk as a gesture of his approval.

Moreau had definitely gone native in his approach to life's little problems. Like food, the Shan regarded sex as something one should share with good friends, not with strangers. If your friend is hungry, you offer him food; if he's horny, you offer him sex, usually with a wife or daughter, assuming, of course, that she agrees, which she usually does. The corollary also applies: if your wife is horny and you can't handle it, you offer her one of your good friends as a substitute. Everyone gets satisfied, no one gets hurt, nobody gets jealous or angry, and best of all, there's nothing to hide.

So for a while there, I had the best of both worlds: Loma's luscious body in the afternoon, and Moreau's dreamy opium at night.

One of my summer chores was to do the fishing. In early spring the tribesmen stocked their ponds and paddies with fresh fish spawn brought down from high mountain streams. When they drained the ponds and paddies in the fall, thousands of fat fish were left flopping in the mud, waiting to be harvested. Most of this harvest was sun-dried or made into fermented fish paste. During the summer, however, we had to do our own fishing upstream, and I enjoyed hiking into the hills to do this job. I liked to fish the mountain streams and little lakes where the Shan gathered spawn in springtime, and my favorite spot was the cool alpine meadow where I'd buried Suraya.

One afternoon, I grabbed my gear and followed the winding trail up to the stream that flows across that magic meadow. As the trail twisted up into the mountains, the tropical jungle thinned and gave way to alpine forest. I heard the waterfall that fed the stream splashing in the distance, and the trees hummed with the sounds of birds and insects feeding and mating.

After paying respects at Suraya's grave, I sat down by the stream for a smoke. I could see fish darting across the smooth stones, breaking water here and there to snap at flies and waterskaters. A cool breeze blew down off the mountains.

The tribesmen's method of fishing is simple and effective. Instead of using hooks and lines, they trap their fish in bamboo baskets, then pull them out of the water by hand. The cone-shaped baskets stand about three feet high, open at both ends. The ribs at the wide end extend a few inches beyond the rim and are sharpened to points.

To fish with this gear, you wade into a pond or stream and stand stock-still with the basket held just above the surface of the water, wide end down. When you see a fish swim by, you simply ram the basket down over it, sinking the spiked ribs into the sand and stones to form a little cage around the fish. Then you reach down through the narrow opening on top, grab the fish with your hand, and toss it into a sack strung from your shoulder. The sack trails in the water to keep the fish inside alive and fresh. It's a lot more efficient than hook and line, and when you get the hang of it, you can sometimes trap two or three fish at once.

I'd always felt a serene sense of solitude in that meadow, but this time, after hauling in my third fish, I began to feel that strange tingling sensation on the back of my neck, indicating that another human energy field was nearby, observing me. I looked around but saw nothing; yet the feeling continued to linger in my gut.

I caught two more fish, then waded back to shore to rest and eat the snacks Loma had packed for me. While I lay stretched out in the grass smoking, the vibrations in my belly suddenly grew so strong that I bolted to my feet and scanned the meadow for an intruder. I could hardly believe my eyes: bounding across the meadow like a kangaroo, raggedy robes flapping in the wind, came a wizened old man with a long, wispy beard, his hair tied up in a topknot. It took him less than ten seconds to cover the ground between us, a distance of at least one hundred fifty yards. He bounced along with no apparent effort, ten yards at a leap.

The old man landed softly on his feet right in front of me, without a trace of breathlessness, and stood there gazing at me. His long hair was bundled up in a knot on the crown of his head in ancient Taoist style, held in place with a chipped jade hairpin. His hair and beard were slightly streaked with gray, and it was clear from the look in his eyes and the way he dressed that he was very old—and that he was Chinese.

"Well! My Heaven!" he boomed at me in formal Mandarin. *"So you are Luo Bao-shan, Master Lee's favorite disciple."* He bowed deeply, then said, *"Do you not remember me?"*

"Ah, no—I mean, yes, I am Luo Bao-shan, and Master Lee was indeed my teacher," I stammered. *"May I please know your esteemed name?"* Still overawed by his amazing flight across the meadow, I could barely speak.

"My unworthy name is Ling Yun." His name jogged my memory. It means "soaring in the clouds." He was Old Lee's friend and fellow Taoist adept, the one Old Lee had taken me to visit long ago in China, where he was living in a cave high up on a mountain outside of Chungking.

"I have observed you here often for more than one year," he said, *"but only today did you feel my presence. That is very good progress. You are slowly but surely recovering your internal powers. Now do you remember me?"*

"Yes, of course I do! I met you with Master Lee in Szechuan during the war. You had retired to the mountains to cultivate Tao. Please forgive my stupidity."

He waved aside my apology, and we sat down in the grass to talk, a bond already forming between us. "*I also like to fish here,*" he said. "*That is how I first discovered you.*" He explained that when the Communists made their final advance into southern China, he and Old Lee and most of Old Lee's students had joined General Duan's exodus into Burma. "*All along we thought that our exile would only be temporary, and that Chiang Kai-shek would soon launch a counterattack from Taiwan. For years we followed General Duan, hoping that our return to China would come soon. Master Lee was very worried about his father, who had remained secluded in China when we escaped. He was much too old to travel and did not wish to die in a foreign land.*" Old Lee's father was the great Taoist adept Lee Ching-yun, who was already 273 years old when I met him in China in 1943.

"*Only when all hope of returning to China had faded did Master Lee decide to leave this place. By that time, most of the Chinese officers in Burma had already turned to the opium trade. One of those officers was Ching Wei, who, as a disciple of Master Lee, invited us to join his band and treated us very well. But Master Lee hated opium and the effects it had on the health and morale of our men. He failed to persuade Ching Wei to continue the fight against Communism in China, for by then Ching Wei was interested only in accumulating personal power and profit.*" Ling Yun reached into my basket and helped himself to a banana.

"*So Master Lee finally left Burma in disgust. But before he left, he instructed Ching Wei to take full responsibility for my welfare. I could not face the prospect of returning to the dusty world, so I decided to retire once again to the mountains, where I could continue to cultivate Tao in peace. Ching Wei felt honored to fulfill his old master's last request, and he gave me an entire mountain for myself, where no one else is permitted to wander. Once or twice a year I request a few basic supplies from him, but my needs here are very simple.*"

"What happened to Master Lee? Where did he go?"

Ling Yun shrugged. "*Perhaps Hong Kong, perhaps Taipei, perhaps America. Who knows? Wherever he is, I'm sure that he is teaching and healing people. That is the difference between him and me. I am a hermit by nature, and I prefer the company of wild animals to that of men; but Master Lee prefers to live among people, where he may teach the Way and manifest the 'benevolent heart, benevolent art' of the healer, curing people of their ills. Even when he was here in the jungle, he always sought students among Ching Wei's men and taught them daily. As for me, I often do not see another human being for nine or ten months at a time."*

I was amazed to meet Ling Yun under those circumstances, and I felt flattered that he'd remembered me. Old Lee had always told me that Ling Yun was one of the most accomplished Taoist adepts in China. *"He can fly to the moon and wander among the stars,"* Old Lee used to tell me, *"and he can run from Chengdu to Chungking in a single day."* I'd never understood what he meant by the latter statement, until I witnessed Ling Yun bounding across the meadow that afternoon.

After talking for a while, I cautiously suggested, *"Perhaps you would be so kind as to teach me some new techniques sometime."*

"Certainly! Master Lee was very fond of you, and he spoke highly of your ability. With the strong foundation in Tao which he gave you and your own determination to advance your practice, anything is possible." He made a strange gesture with his hands and muttered a mantra. *"It is always such a pleasure to meet a fellow traveler on the path of Tao. Today, men seem interested only in money, intoxicants, and women. It has been a long time since I have met anyone with whom I could discuss the Mysterious Arts. Yes, I will teach you, but first you must come see where I live."* He rose to his feet from a cross-legged posture in a single smooth movement, then clasped his hands and stretched his arms up to the sky until his spine crackled like popcorn. *"Now that you have done the fishing, I need not bother with that!"* He laughed and beckoned me to follow him.

We hiked up a steep ravine toward a craggy mountain that towered against the sky. I had trouble keeping up with Ling Yun as he skipped lightly along the trail, and I was wheezing by the time we broke through the forest onto a small plateau only a few hundred feet below the peak of the mountain. Until then, I thought I was in good shape, but compared to Ling Yun, I moved like a lumbering ox.

A large cave yawned from the face of the mountain. Near it, a small spring trickled down through cracks in the rock, forming a little pool, which then drained into a rivulet. Ling Yun bounded up to a stone ledge that formed a kind of terrace in front of his cave.

"*Sit here,*" he said, indicating a circle of smooth stones set around a blackened fire pit. He disappeared into the cave and came back out with an old earthenware kettle, a box of herbs, and a couple of clay cups. "*First, we shall drink tea,*" he announced, squatting down to stir the embers of his morning fire and blow it back to life. He ambled over to the spring to fill the kettle with water, then stuffed it with a variety of dried herbs and set it on the fire to boil.

"*As you know, Master Lee and I both follow the Internal School of Tao, and we studied together under several masters in our youth. But I also practice the Secret Doctrine of Tibet—the Diamond Way. Though I cleave closely to the Taoist view of life, I have discovered many useful spiritual practices in the tantric teachings of Tibet. As for Master Lee, he followed his father's path as an herbalist and healer, and devoted himself to cultivating the arts of health and longevity.*"

He picked up a large dry tree leaf and used it to fan the fire. "*I have always preferred living alone in the mountains. I cannot bear towns and cities for more than a few days at a time. For me, this simple cave is more comfortable than the grandest palace. That is why I decided not to accompany Master Lee back to the civilized world.*" The kettle bubbled to a boil, and a powerful aroma filled the air. He removed it from the fire with bare hands and poured out two cups. It tasted a bit like licorice.

We talked for hours about martial arts, herbal medicine, Taoist alchemy, and other esoteric subjects of interest only to practicing Taoists. I hadn't enjoyed a conversation like that since my days in China with Old Lee. Ling Yun's accomplishments were impressive: he could beam energy from the palms of his hands, project his spirit from his body, and anticipate events by clairvoyance. He'd also mastered the ancient Tibetan skill of generating *tum-mo*, the "fire in the belly," a breathing practice that could keep a man warm as toast while he sat meditating naked in the snow. At times, Ling Yun subsisted on nothing but a few cups of water and a handful of barley a day. None of this had anything to do with magic, nor was there anything particularly mysterious about it. They're all genuine powers that require the utmost discipline and the deepest dedication to cultivate. Ordinary people simply don't have the time and patience for it.

I asked him how he had hopped across the meadow that afternoon.

"Ah, that is what the Tibetans call lung-gom: *it means 'wind leaping.' In ancient times, Tibetan lamas cultivated this skill for traveling swiftly between distant monasteries across the harsh terrain of their frozen land. There are no roads in Tibet, and ordinary travel is therefore extremely slow and difficult there, even for pack animals. So the lamas developed lung-gom as a means of leaping across the land like the wind, using their astral bodies to propel their physical bodies. I find it very useful here in the mountains*".

He stood up, flared his nostrils, and drew in a big breath of air, puffing up like a bullfrog. Rolling his eyes up into his head so that only the whites showed, he exhaled with a long hiss and said, "*Watch!*" Standing in a low crouch, he sucked in another big breath and, with no apparent effort, leaped high into the air, propelling himself in a long graceful arc from the ledge out to the middle of the clearing below, a distance of at least thirty yards. He waved at me and laughed, then leaped back to the ledge with equal ease, landing softly beside me. "*It is simply a matter of summoning forth the will to shift command of the body from the temporal human mind over to the luminous immortal spirit, then focusing intent to move the astral body like the wind. The body of flesh then follows like a shadow. Come, let us try it together!*"

I protested that I was not trained for that sort of thing, but he pulled me up to my feet anyway and stood me opposite him, pressing his palms tightly against mine. He chugged a few deep breaths, and suddenly I felt something like hot molten metal stream from his palms into mine, then flow up my arms and circulate throughout my whole body, binding us together in an unbreakable embrace of energy. I could not move a muscle.

Ling Yun rolled up his eyes, filled his lungs, and as he exhaled, he yelled, "*Leap!*" I felt an enormous magnetic force pull us both up into the air in perfect tandem, and we sailed smoothly over to the same spot in the clearing. The sensation reminded me of the initial moments of free fall when jumping from an airplane, but the landing was much gentler than touching down with a parachute. He immediately repeated the process, and we flew back to the ledge. The moment he released my palms from his, my knees buckled and I collapsed on the ground.

He roared with laughter and pointed at my pants. They were soaked.

"Scared the piss out of you, did I? Never mind! Once your body grows accustomed to the sensation of relinquishing control to your spirit, that will no longer happen. Fear resides in the kidneys, and that is why the bladder empties when the ordinary human mind feels frightened. But soon your mind will no longer fear the feeling of relinquishing control of your body and allowing spirit to command instead. Your energy pulse is strong and stable, so you should have no trouble cultivating these powers yourself. But it will take time and practice. Once you have learned to subordinate your body and mind to the command of energy and spirit, you will find yourself capable of remarkable things." I felt thoroughly drained—more from fright than effort—but a few sips of his herbal brew immediately revived me.

Ling Yun told me that he'd encountered Old Lee several times in recent years while practicing dream yoga. *"But I did not recognize the location, so I cannot tell you where he is. Identifying a place in dream travel is almost impossible unless you have already been to that place in person. If you have been there before in your physical body, then something in the dreamscape will always provide a familiar hint that stimulates your memory of that place. But I can tell you this much for certain: Master Lee is living somewhere along the Magic Meridian."*

"Magic Meridian?"

He explained that the earth's electromagnetic energy flows along well-defined channels, just as our own energy flows through specific meridians in the body. Like human meridians, certain of the earth's energy channels transmit far more energy than others and function as powerful conductors. The Tropic of Cancer, he said, is one of the planet's most powerful conductors of electromagnetic energy, and that's why it's known as the earth's Magic Meridian.

"The Magic Meridian is the most beneficial belt of land in which to live on this planet. It amplifies the vital energy of anyone who lives within its field and thereby promotes health and longevity. That is why Ching Wei chose this location for his kingdom. He too has studied these matters. He views this meridian as a powerful celestial dragon coiled around the earth, and so he named this place Dragon Mountain. Ever since the dawn of Chinese civilization five thousand years ago, the dragon has been the enduring symbol of emperors and sages alike, for the dragon embodies wisdom and power in perfect harmony."

He poured out the last of the tea and continued his explanation. "The Magic Meridian can greatly facilitate dream travel from one point to another anywhere along its path. It carries your spirit along like a leaf in the wind while your body sleeps. That is why I'm sure Master Lee lives somewhere along this belt. Otherwise I would not have encountered his presence so readily in my dream wandering." Later, when I looked at a map, I noted with great interest that the Tropic of Cancer runs from Dragon Mountain in northern Burma straight across southern China to the Straits of Formosa, then crosses smack-dab through the middle of Taiwan. So perhaps Old Lee was there. Tracing the Tropic of Cancer further east across the map, I noticed another interesting thing: it runs straight through the so-called Bermuda Triangle in the Caribbean Sea. Maybe that explains some of the strange phenomena that aircraft flying through that region so frequently encounter.

Suddenly Ling Yun stood up and rubbed his hands together. "All this talk has made me hungry. Before you return to the village, we must eat." He took two fish from my basket, leaving three for me to take back home. He cleaned them with an odd-looking tool, rubbed them inside and out with salt, stuffed them with some fresh herbs he kept hanging at the mouth of his cave, and skewered them over the coals. We watched the fish cook and ate them in silence. Once again I felt the herbs he used give me a distinct boost of energy.

As I gathered my gear and prepared to leave, Ling Yun dictated a list of things he wanted me to bring back for him on my next visit: matches, Chinese tea, some flour and barley, and a variety of rare medicinal herbs to be procured from a Chinese pharmacy in Bangkok. *"Oh yes, and don't forget to bring me six bottles of French brandy,"* he added.

"Brandy?"

"Yes, I steep wild tonic herbs in it to make medicinal wines, precisely in accordance with Master Lee's formulas. I like the taste of French brandy. I grew accustomed to it when Master Lee and I were living with Ching Wei. He will provide it."

He accompanied me to the edge of the plateau and bade me farewell at the top of the trail. *"When may I come visit you again?"* I asked, expecting him to say "tomorrow" or "next week" or something like that.

But instead he said, *"Come back after three months. From tomorrow until then, the only place you will find me is soaring in the clouds! I have much to do and far to go."* His laughter echoed through the valley as he waved me down the trail.

I turned to bid him a final farewell and saw the profile of his head, topknot skewered with jade pin, etched in silhouette against the darkening sky. Suddenly I felt like Ronald Coleman in that old movie, *The Lost Horizon*, when he reluctantly says goodbye to his newfound friends as he leaves Shangri-la. Already I longed to return.

XIX

It caused quite a stir in Poong when early one morning, Ching Wei's men returned to Dragon Mountain with a group of five new captives, two of them women. These were the first white women ever to set foot there, and the tribesmen trampled each other's toes and craned their necks to get a good look. Never before had they seen women with such long blond hair and big blue eyes, such lanky legs and buxom breasts, and their imaginations ran wild as they ogled the new arrivals.

The platoon had stumbled into their camp in northern Thailand, en route back from one of Ching Wei's forward supply depots there. They were young Americans, all in their early twenties, and they'd been trekking near the Golden Triangle. Normally, his troops would have ignored these kids, but recently Ching Wei's passion for collecting "foreign guests" had become so compulsive that the captain figured he'd earn a few extra points by hauling the five of them back to Dragon Mountain as a surprise for the Boss.

I was smoking under a bodhi tree in the village when I heard the commotion. *"Step back! Make way!"* Captain Lu shouted at the gathering crowd. Tired and irritable, he fired a burst of gunshots into the air to clear a path through the gawkers, scaring his captives half to death.

He led his prize over to the communal pavilion and barked at them in Chinese. "*Sit here and wait!*" Then he jabbed a finger at three of his men. "*Watch them well and keep these village dogs away!*" He dismissed the rest of the squad and trotted up the trail to the palace to report his catch to Ching Wei.

Bedraggled and frightened after the long march across the border from Thailand, the newcomers sat in sullen silence, surrounded by a curious crowd of villagers. The three guys looked like typical college kids from California—sun-bleached hair, nice tans, faded blue jeans, peace signs and other insignia patched to their packs. One of them wore a UCLA Bruins football jersey. The two gals were both raving beauties. One had blond hair and blue eyes and was dressed in a tight beige jumpsuit that hugged her curves like a glove. The other had long auburn hair, big doe eyes, and breasts as firm and round as grapefruits. Both were tall and well built. Pretty soon I too was craning my neck to get a better look.

The crowd gawked and gossiped for a while, but when it came time to head out to the hills and fields to work, most of the adults dispersed, leaving just a few old men and small children hanging around to gape. I felt sorry for those kids; they were scared witless by their ordeal and had no idea where they were or why. The auburn pulled a canteen from her pack and raised it to her lips, but it was bone dry. She tossed it angrily to the ground, then buried her face in her hands and started sobbing.

I went over to the store, bought a six-pack of chilled beer, and sat down beside them. "*Get away from them, you muddled egg!*" a short, young Chinese guard shouted at me. He raised his rifle and brandished it in my face.

"*Shut your filthy dog's lips and turn that gun away, or else I'll fire it up your stinking ass!*" I snapped back at him, standing up to emphasize my point. "*Shall I inform the Boss that you threaten the life of his friend and pilot?*" This outburst surprised and confused the young recruit, for he was new and had never seen me before. Then one of the older guards whispered something in his ear, and he immediately changed his tune and began to apologize, which goes to show how much clout I had around Poong by then. A couple of Shan oldsters snickered at the guard's humiliation, so he tried to restore face by kicking them clear across the plaza.

"Care for a cold one?" I said, offering them each a beer as I sat down next to the auburn. "My name's Jack."

They stared at me in utter amazement, then looked at the frosty cans and yelped with delight. "All right, man. Far out!" they chimed. "Too much!" The familiar whoosh as they popped open the tabs on their beer cans must have sounded like a comforting call from home. Things couldn't be all that bad where cold beer's to be had.

Refreshed, they relaxed a bit and introduced themselves: John, Tom, Bobby, Vicki, and Laura. I never did find out their last names. First they wanted to know where they were and why, so I filled them in. I told them about Ching Wei and his merry menagerie of white guests, which by that time numbered around three hundred, and I tried to describe life at Dragon Mountain.

"Holy shit! You mean we've been brought here as part of this guy's private zoo?"

"Something like that. Like all zoos, you get well fed and well cared for, but you're not allowed to run away." They blanched when I told them what happened to people who tried to escape. It felt strange talking to them like that, as if I were an old counselor welcoming a new batch of kids to summer camp.

"Uh, what about us?" auburn Laura wanted to know. "What does he do with the women he brings here?"

"Relax. He doesn't have a taste for white women. He's got his own harem full of Asian women, and when it comes to sex, his appetite runs strictly Asian." I didn't try to explain Ching Wei's fetish for white tigers and their bald "orchids," because I thought it might offend the girls. "In fact, you're the first white girls ever brought here. The patrol picked you up on its own initiative, not on Ching Wei's orders. They figured it would please him, and they're probably right. As far as he's concerned, the more the merrier."

Laura and Vicki looked relieved to hear that their visions of rape and mayhem were unlikely to come true. I especially liked Laura, and I promised myself to try to get closer to her later.

We went through another six-pack of beer before Captain Lu returned to fetch his prize. He was all puffed up with pride and growled at the guards, *"The Boss wants to see them. Now! Take them up to the palace. Now!"* I reassured them again that Ching Wei was a civilized man and would treat them well—if they behaved.

As time went by, Ching Wei grew ever more perverse. Before, he would have punished his men for abducting anyone without specific orders from him, but instead he now rewarded them with gold ingots and extra rations from the store. His officers all wanted a piece of the action, so new captives were dragged in almost every month.

The first thing Ching Wei did when those five kids were brought before him was to have the two girls stripped stark naked. As Laura told me later, "He inspected us up real close and sniffed at our bodies from head to foot, as if we were flowers in a greenhouse, but he never laid a hand on either of us. He gives me the creeps!"

According to Hoffmann, Ching Wei's drug habit was also getting out of hand. The shrapnel in his liver had shifted position again, inducing such intense pain and erratic mood changes that he had to increase his dosage sharply. That meant his supply of China White was running out faster than anticipated, a matter of deep concern to Ching Wei. It also meant that his drug addled mind prompted him to increasingly bizarre behavior, a matter of deep concern to us all.

As a fresh distraction, Ching Wei instituted a new form of entertainment at his courtyard parties. He started staging fights to the death between two men he wished to punish, or between men and vicious animals from his zoo, like gladiators in a Roman circus. The first time I witnessed one of these bloody spectacles was at his Mid-Autumn Moon Festival celebration in September 1977.

The invitations stated that we should appear in the courtyard promptly at noon. No one was late. There was the usual arrangement of chairs, with a table for hors d'oeuvres and attractive young girls serving drinks. But this time there was a new feature: a circular cage of steel, about thirty feet in diameter and ten feet high, stood in the middle of the courtyard. Huddled on the ground in chains sat five frightened men: two whites, two Shan, and one Chinese.

"You will enjoy today's program," Ching Wei assured me over a glass of champagne. His eyes gleamed with chemical pleasure.

"Suffering and death don't turn me on," I replied frankly.

"But suffering and death are as natural as pleasure and life itself!" he insisted. "There can be no pleasure in life without suffering, and nothing gives me greater pleasure than someone else's suffering. And among life's greatest pleasures of all, none can compare with the well-staged spectacle of another man's death." He threw his head back and brayed with laughter, crazy as a loon. I took advantage of his good mood to ask him about the young American trekkers his men had brought in.

"Ah, yes, delightful young people," he said. "So fresh and so full of energy. They are a welcome addition to my community. And since they have come as a group with two women, they may share a house together in Poong. That way, the women will be safe from some of my more barbaric guests."

"They're bound to try to escape."

His face darkened. "That would be very foolish! And fatal! You have warned them of the consequences?"

"Of course, I warned them. But like you said, they're young and full of energy, not burnt out like the rest of us. Young people don't worry much about death. What about the two girls?"

"Very attractive, but unfortunately, foreign women do not suit my taste." Not only did Ching Wei prefer bald pudenda, he found the smell of white flesh repugnant. "Captain Lu, the officer who brought them here, has asked me for possession of the golden-haired girl. So far I have refused him. Please assure the young ladies that they will not be molested here, but they must under no circumstances attempt to use their charms to solicit favors from my guards or to attempt escape."

"What about me? May your honorable pilot make a play for their charms? After all, I helped you bag Colonel Hsu."

"Ho! So that's it! You want the white girls for yourself!" Ching Wei grinned knowingly. "How very interesting. Ever since you lost your woman in Poong, you have lived like a monk." He knew nothing about my affair with Moreau's wife. "Perhaps one of these girls will help revive your spirits. And you have indeed been of great service to me. You may therefore do as you wish with them."

The roar of a tiger rumbled across the courtyard, cutting short our conversation. Cramped inside a small cage that had just been rolled in from the zoo was an irate and very hungry Bengal tiger.

"Come, everyone, please be seated," Ching Wei announced, taking his usual place in the middle.

The spectacle that followed typified Ching Wei's perverse cruelty. First, he had two Shan tribesmen lashed together by their left wrists and shoved inside the cage. Slender, razor sharp blades were then placed in their right hands. The two men came from adjacent villages, Ching Wei explained, and had been feuding over the same piece of paddy for years. When their feud erupted in violence and threatened village harmony—not to mention delaying the opium harvest—the two village sawbwas had brought the matter to Ching Wei's attention. And this was his way of settling the problem: the winner would get the land, and the loser would be buried beneath it as fertilizer.

At first, the two men circled each other warily, bug-eyed with fear, sweat beading on their brows, blades poised to strike as their lashed wrists trembled with tension. Suddenly, they both started flailing their blades wildly at each other, hacking chunks of flesh from each other's arms, gashing face and head, howling and cussing. The battle lasted far too long for anyone's comfort, and even Ching Wei began to fidget, though more from boredom than aversion. No decisive blow was ever struck. Instead, one of the men eventually bled to death and collapsed in a pool of blood.

The winner wasn't left in much better shape.

By that time, the tiger had caught the scent of blood, and the whole courtyard echoed with his ravenous roars. Ching Wei ordered the two white men tossed inside the cage, armed with heavy cudgels. They stood quaking against the bars as the tiger was released inside, and one of those poor bastards fainted on the spot with fright.

The tiger roared and bounded at the other man, who caught the beast square on the snout with a blow from his cudgel, temporarily stunning it. Frothing with rage, the tiger circled swiftly and leaped again, sinking its jaws into the man's neck and twisting him to the ground like a rag doll.

In the meantime, the other guy revived, just in time to see the tiger tear out the other man's jugular. With a blood curdling war whoop, he attacked the feeding tiger from behind, bashing it on the head with his cudgel. The cat spun around and screeched. With a single swift swipe, it clawed open the man's abdomen, spilling his guts onto the flagstone. For a moment, the man just stood there, watching his bowels unravel on the ground, face frozen in surprise. Then he collapsed and the tiger took out his throat. Ching Wei never did tell us what these guys had done to incur his wrath.

As the tiger fed on the corpses, an enormous elephant was led into the courtyard for the grand finale. A smooth round rock about the size of a watermelon was placed on the ground in front of us. The final victim was dragged over and stretched out so that his head rested on the stone's surface. He was a Chinese guard who'd been caught sound asleep at his post after smoking opium on duty, and he pleaded pathetically for mercy as the guards held him down. The zookeeper maneuvered the elephant up to the stone, then jabbed it behind the ear with a long, barbed stick. The elephant automatically raised a foot and held it hovering over the man's head.

"It has taken several years to train the elephant to perform this trick on command," Ching Wei told us. "Actually, the method is based on traditional Chinese acupuncture, applied to animals. I first encountered this technique in India during the war. It is very colorful to witness, and actually quite painless for the victim."

He sat down and nodded at the zookeeper, who yanked the barbed point from the vital spot behind the elephant's ear, causing the animal to drop its poised foot onto the man's head. It popped like a pumpkin, with a sound that was every bit as sickening as the sight. I almost retched. When it was over, Ching Wei ordered the guards to feed all the corpses to the tigers in the zoo, except for the tribesman who was to be buried as fertilizer. Then he led us inside his palace for a lavish banquet to celebrate the Mid-Autumn Moon Festival.

The banquet ended promptly at 10:00 PM. In his growing paranoia, Ching Wei no longer invited guests to stay all night for orgies in his palace. Between midnight and dawn, only his guards, women, and Dr. Hoffmann were permitted inside the palace grounds.

Though I'd drunk a lot of champagne, I felt remarkably clear as I strolled back to the village. My exercise regimen had greatly increased my tolerance for intoxicants. A bright harvest moon hung high in a starry sky, and moonbeams trickled down through the trees, mottling the trail in shades of silver.

The village lay sound asleep, except for the bar, where lights still blazed inside. Everything stood etched in clear detail in the milky moonlight, and the bodhi trees cast big, black patches on the ground. Suddenly I noticed the tip of a cigarette glowing beneath my favorite bodhi tree. As I approached, a familiar voice greeted me from the shadow.

"Nice night. Never seen such a big beautiful moon." It was lanky, luscious Laura, sitting there all by herself.

"That's what the Chinese call the Mid-Autumn Moon. They say it's the biggest, brightest moon of the year. Today's the festival to celebrate it." I sat down next to her and lit a cigarette, catching a brief glimpse of her face in the match flame. "What are you doing out here so late?"

"Same as you, enjoying a stroll in the moonlight. Do you always wear that costume?" she asked, rubbing her hand across my Chinese robe. "Real silk. Feels nice."

"Just came down from one of Ching Wei's banquets. We're all expected to wear these outfits up there. Sometimes he reminds me of a mad Hollywood director, forever conjuring up elaborate scenes that only he understands and appreciates. We're his cast of thousands."

Her laughter pealed like chimes in the night air. "He sounds like a real kook to me. This whole place is weird, like a lost world full of lost people, run by a maniac who's lost his mind. I've watched some pretty strange characters coming in and out of that bar tonight."

"You'd best keep out of there," I advised. We talked some more, and I suggested a walk up the hill to Moreau's place. "From my veranda you can see the whole village and all of Dragon Mountain. It should be beautiful in this moonlight."

That appealed to her, so we stood up and stepped out of the shadow of the tree. I noticed that she wore a faded old U.C. Berkeley sweatshirt.

"I went to Berkeley myself for a few years before the war," I told her as we walked up to Moreau's. "But I never graduated." She thought I meant the Vietnam War. When I told her I was talking about World War II, she tittered and made me tell her all about campus life at Berkeley in 1940.

We tiptoed barefoot onto the veranda, in order not to awaken Moreau and his family. The entire landscape glowed in the moonlight, with Dragon Mountain looming against the star-studded sky like the sail of a giant ship in the night. A few pinpoints of orange light still flickered through the windows of Ching Wei's palace. Laura purred with pleasure at the view.

"I heard you come in," Moreau slurred, shuffling onto the veranda. It was a holiday and he did not have to go to work the following morning, so he was celebrating the Moon Festival by smoking his best grade opium. "A beautiful night, no? Tonight I am smoking la crème de la crème, a special gift from Ching Wei. It has been aging in his cellar for over five years. Would you care to join me for a few pipes?" He still hadn't noticed Laura sitting in the shadows.

"Sure, why not! Just the thing to top off a pleasant evening. Mind if my friend here joins us?" I lit a match and introduced Moreau to Laura.

"Mais, bien sûr!" Moreau blurted with more energy than I'd heard him muster in years. "Comme belle jeune fille! C'est mon plaisir," he burbled, planting a kiss on her hand. "Please, come inside."

He led us into his den, tripping over the doorjamb as he entered. Like a big, tired bird returning to its nest, he lay his head onto the wooden block with an immense sigh of relief. I put out a couple of blocks for Laura and myself, and we lay down with our heads toward the lamp.

"Ever smoke opium before?" I asked her. "This is the real thing."

"Far out!" she chirped. "I've always wanted to try this."

While Moreau busied himself cleaning the pipe and cooking the opium, I explained the method of smoking to Laura and pulled out the vial of cocaine I always kept in Moreau's stash box for these occasions.

"Oh, wow!" she beamed. "Coke, too! This must really be my lucky night!" I sniffed up a few snorts of the stuff and handed the vial to her. She needed no instruction on how to handle that. While we waited, I explained Hoffmann's theory about the Yin and Yang of drugs, which intrigued her to no end.

Moreau loaded the pipe, and we began to smoke in earnest. A beneficial side effect of sniffing a bit of cocaine before smoking is that some of the crystals fly down your throat and numb the nerves there, enabling you to inhale long and deep on the pipe without gagging. By the third round, Laura had mastered the method and was smoking each cone down to its final flicker.

"Feels fine," she cooed, letting Moreau slip the pipe from her hands to reload it. "Kind of like floating on a cloud." Moreau enjoyed nothing better than introducing someone new to the delights of his favorite habit, and he beamed at her favorable response.

We smoked and talked and drifted for a few hours, wispy clouds of opium curling lazily above our heads. From time to time,

Laura and I fortified ourselves with a snort of cocaine. Finally, Moreau's eyes fell shut and his jaw hung slack, and I knew that he'd lie there without stirring until late next morning, cradling his precious pipe like a baby.

    I pulled Laura up by the hand and quietly took her into my room. Without a word, she drew her sweatshirt up over her head and tossed it aside, then posed in the candlelight. After all these years with Asian women, I'd completely forgotten what pink nipples looked like. She did not resist when I peeled off her jeans and buried myself inside her.

XX

When we awoke late next morning, she crouched on top of me, and we made love again. Then I began to worry about Moreau's wife and what she would think of the situation. I envisioned jealous pouting, snide remarks, racial tension. But once again I was thinking like a white man instead of a tribesman.

We emerged from my room to find a hearty breakfast of coffee, fresh fruit, hot pastries, and tupa waiting for us out on the veranda. While we ate, Loma prepared hot water for Laura's morning bath. My daughter bounded in to say good morning, stared shyly at Laura, then raced out to the garden, where she turned her head again to marvel at Laura's foreign features.

"That's my daughter, Shana," I told Laura. "Her mother was Shan." No further explanation seemed necessary, nor was any demanded.

"She's adorable!"

"Maybe you could teach her to speak some English. She speaks nothing but Shan with me."

"I'd love to! I'll teach her to read and write as well."

After breakfast, Loma took Laura firmly in hand and marched her into the washroom, where she made her strip down and climb into a steaming hot bath. First she gave her a long luxurious shampoo, followed by a bracing head and neck massage, then stood her up for a complete body wash. Loma clucked with wonder at Laura's buxom breasts and pert pink nipples, and the curly thatch of chestnut hair between her legs. She'd never seen a white woman before, dressed or naked, and she didn't stop scrubbing Laura until her curiosity was thoroughly satisfied. No doubt Laura's body would now become a topic of gossip down in the village market. Laura felt flattered by all the attention, and by the end of the day the two women were good friends. No pouting, no shouting, no nasty looks.

Since it was a holiday, Loma was planning a special meal that evening, and she invited Laura to stay over for another night. While Loma shopped and cooked, Laura and I spent the rest of the day sitting in the garden and making love in my room.

That was the start of a very pleasant relationship. Laura came up to the house several days a week to give Shana English lessons, and she usually ended up spending the night there as well. She sewed clothes and made a charming rag doll for Shana. When Laura wasn't around, Loma and I continued our affair as happily as ever. We had the best of East and West in our little household, but outside things went from bad to worse.

By the spring of 1978, Ching Wei's troops were skirmishing frequently with both the Burmese Communists and the Thai army. As usual, the issue was opium, not politics. Since entering the opium business, the Bur-Coms had been trading a lot of their stock with Ching Wei in exchange for rice, fuel, medicine, and other vital supplies. Within Ching Wei's domain, all the villages were prosperous, and they consistently produced a surplus of everything. By contrast, villages under Communist control never produced enough of anything, especially food. Even in the jungles of Burma, free enterprise seemed to work a lot better than Communism.

Increasingly desperate for cash and supplies, the Communists kept raising the price of the raw opium they sold to Ching Wei, who never liked dealing with them in the first place. Finally, he got fed up with their gouging and sent his own agents into

Communist-controlled villages up north to purchase raw opium directly from the growers there. Ching Wei always paid the peasants a much better price for opium than the Communists did, and he always paid in cash, rather than the worthless credit chits the Bur-Coms always gave them. Before long, Ching Wei was siphoning off a major cut of the opium harvest in the Communist-held Kachen Hills.

    I knew a couple of the Chinese officers in charge of Ching Wei's operations in the Kachen Hills, and they gave me quite a bit of information on Bur-Com troop strength and movements there. It seems that we've seriously underestimated their numbers and commitment to their cause, while overestimating their firepower and political influence in the region. Losing logistical support from Peking dealt them a heavy blow, and their top priority was acquisition of new weapons and ammunition. Recently a few Soviet agents were spotted up there, indicating that the KGB may be trying to fill the vacuum left by Peking's abrupt withdrawal of support, but frankly I doubt that any outside power will ever exercise any decisive influence over the Shan, Karen, Wa, and other hill tribes in northern Burma. They are too ancient, too traditional, and far too set in their ways to be controlled by outsiders. The best policy would be to simply leave them alone.

    Firefights between Ching Wei's caravans and Communist patrols grew more frequent and intense throughout the year. In once incident, Bur-Coms trapped a unit of Ching Wei's men in a remote ravine and slaughtered forty-six of them, including one of his top field commanders. The two tons of opium they had just purchased in the Kachen Hills were lost, and only a dozen survivors managed to straggle back to Dragon Mountain alive.

    This infuriated Ching Wei and made him hot for revenge. But in his usual inscrutable way, he pretended at first to overlook the incident. Acting as though he'd learned a bitter lesson, he stopped buying opium from villages in Communist territory and resumed buying it from the Bur-Coms at their own inflated prices.

    Then one day, the news came in that over one hundred Bur-Com troops in three different camps had died of food poisoning. Ching Wei had laced thirty sacks of rice bound for the

Communists with strychnine. He got his revenge, and needless to say, the Burmese Communists never again traded with him. Instead, they began refining their opium into heroin and trading it for weapons and other supplies with major dealers in Bangkok and Penang. A lot of those weapons turned out to be American leftovers from Vietnam, still in mint condition.

About that time, Ching Wei suffered another major setback. The formerly cooperative Thai military command abruptly stopped protecting his operations in northern Thailand. With Uncle Sam threatening to cut off military aid and suspend trade credits to Thailand, Bangkok finally decided to crack down on heroin traffic from Burma. The Thais began shuffling their military commanders in the northern provinces so frequently that Ching Wei no longer knew who to pay off.

In July, nine Thai soldiers were killed in a skirmish with Ching Wei's troops that took place well within the Thai side of the border. That was simply too much for Bangkok. They immediately dispatched two thousand Thai Rangers to the north in order to terminate Ching Wei's operations on Thai soil. But Bangkok is so riddled with Ching Wei's moles that they gave him a full week's notice of the impending raid. I had to make six round-trip flights in three days to evacuate all his men and supplies from the airstrip he kept in northern Thailand for his opium deliveries. By the time the Rangers got there, they found nothing but a sleepy little hamlet full of blank faces.

Ching Wei moved the Thai end of his operations down to a new stronghold that straddled the Thai-Burma border about two hundred fifty miles south of Dragon Mountain. He fortified the little village there and cleared a patch of jungle for an airstrip. This time, however, he was completely on his own. After seven years of flying the old route with implicit Thai consent, I now had to familiarize myself with a new route that was hostile from both sides. Neither One-Eye nor I relished the thought of flying through a gauntlet of Thai antiaircraft fire on one side and Bur-Com guns on the other.

In August, Ching Wei disappeared on another one of his business trips to Bangkok and other cities in Southeast Asia.

After the recent shakeup in Bangkok, he needed to establish a new network of connections in order to market and move his products.

"What about his drug habit?" I asked Hoffmann. "How the hell does he handle that on these outside trips?"

"He doesn't. He purges his system of all narcotic drugs before traveling abroad. Of course, he must endure considerable pressure and pain from his liver on these journeys, which is why he usually keeps them short. But whenever the pain becomes unbearable, he uses perfectly legal prescriptions of Demerol and other pharmaceutical painkillers to control it. These offer a small measure of relief, but they provide him no pleasure whatsoever."

"He just kicks the habit like that, cold turkey?"

"Bah! Drug withdrawal as depicted in American movies and storybooks—this so-called 'cold turkey'—is entirely pointless and unnecessary. Detoxification is as simple as Yin and Yang. On the first day of withdrawal, I administer his usual dosage of heroin and cocaine in equal portions. The second day, I reduce the dosage of cocaine by twenty percent but maintain the same dosage of China White. Thus the body is fooled into feeling that it has actually received a dose of heroin twenty percent stronger than the previous day."

"Clever."

"On the third day, the heroin is reduced by twenty percent, but not the cocaine, thereby restoring the relative balance of both drugs used on the first day, except that now the quantity of both drugs has been reduced by twenty percent. On the fourth day, cocaine is again cut by twenty percent, making the relative effect of the heroin feel twenty percent stronger than the day before. The next day, I again cut the heroin by twenty percent, once again restoring the original relative balance of both drugs, but at an actual dosage that is now forty percent less than on the first day. And so I gradually reduce the dosage of each drug on alternate days, while always maintaining their relative balance, until both drugs are entirely eliminated from the system. On the tenth day, I administer a placebo of pure glucose and vitamins. Since the body responds only to the relative balance of drugs in the system, it does not feel the actual dosage levels being gradually reduced and their residues eliminated from the body. Thus there occurs no physical discomfort, no craving for drugs, and none of this stupid 'cold turkey.'"

"If it's so easy to kick a heroin habit, then why do they always make such a big deal about it?"

"Because they don't want people to know how easy it is. They want people to be afraid of it. If people knew the truth about the medical properties of opiates, no one would ever buy pharmaceutical drugs again, because opium alone could replace at least seventy-five percent of the expensive synthetic substitutes provided by the pharmaceutical industry today, at only about one-tenth the cost to the consumer. It is prohibited not because it is a dangerous drug, but because it is such a marvelous medicine for so many conditions and it cannot be patented. Today, the pharmaceutical industry is a four-hundred-billion-dollar-a-year business precisely because opium is banned: it is nothing more or less than a legally condoned drug cartel against whom we compete with a superior product! And since our product works better than theirs, people who need such medicine will buy it at any cost and any risk. If opium were legal, not only would the American pharmaceutical industry collapse, so would our own business. Let's hope the authorities never awaken to this fact!"

I grew attached to Laura. She had Shana chattering freely in English in less than a year, and she seemed to love my daughter as much as I did. Shana treated Laura like a mother, and no doubt she recognized reflections of her own mixed blood in Laura's foreign features. But I knew that Laura still harbored hopes of finding her way back home, despite her apparent contentment. The fact that she and the guy named Tom were on-and-off lovers further complicated the situation.

Sometimes she'd bolt upright in bed at night and say, "I don't want to spend the rest of my life rotting away in this stinking jungle! How on earth can you continue living here year after year, working for that creep? I can't stand it any more: we *must* find a way out of here!" Then she'd burst into tears. This scene always followed the same old script.

"Just be patient a little longer," I'd say. "We'll get out of here eventually. At the rate he's going, Ching Wei can't last forever. Sooner or later he'll die of an overdose, or get himself stabbed in the back, and then we'll fly out of here together and go back home to California." But my forecast of a happy ending sounded as phony to me as it did to her.

"Bullshit, Jack! The only way we'll ever get out of here is to run for it. Tom and Bobby are great mountaineers. They've both been through survival camp in the Rockies. Together we can make it!"

"The Rockies! For crying out loud, Laura, this is the Shan Plateau in northern Burma, not a campground in the Rockies! You don't have wild headhunters, man-eating tigers, and armed bandits running around loose in the Rockies. You'd never even make it to the border."

And so it went, month after month, but I never fully realized how serious she was about getting out of there.

They made their break in early October, right after the monsoon. Pretending to go out for a casual stroll to shop or visit friends, they each took off in a different direction one morning, then headed for a prearranged rendezvous in the jungle, where they'd been stashing supplies for some time. No one even noticed them missing until midmorning the following day, when the old woman assigned to bring them breakfast showed up to find their hut abandoned.

It took less than ten minutes for the news to reach Ching Wei, and only five for his guards to find me and hustle me up to the palace.

"Where are they!" Ching Wei demanded. The veins on his neck throbbed with rage.

"Who?" I wasn't faking it. The guards had told me nothing.

He gave me a hard backhand across the face, and his guards tensed, watching for my reaction. But I just stood there and said nothing.

"Your American friends! They have tried to escape! Where did they go?"

I reeled at the news, and Ching Wei noted the genuine surprise on my face.

"I have no idea," I said. "Had I known they were planning something this stupid, I would have stopped them, but they told me nothing. They're as good as dead now." The thought of Ching Wei's men hunting them down like wild animals made me sick.

"Yes, they are indeed 'dead ducks,' as you say in America. *Anyone who attempts to escape from life in heaven deserves the bitter taste of death in hell.*' But I will spare the girl for you if you simplify matters by telling me their plans. Which way did they go?"

"I wish I knew, but I don't. Like I said, they told me nothing."

He was trying to use Laura's life as a bargaining chip to find out if they'd confided their plans to me in advance, which would have made me an accomplice to their escape. Had I known anything at all about it, I think I would have told him, just in order to save Laura, but I didn't have a clue about their plans. They were goners now, and there was nothing I could do to save them from their fates. Laura had all but spelled out their intentions during our bedtime arguments, but I'd been too blind and complacent to see.

Every time someone tried to escape from Dragon Mountain, Ching Wei took it as a personal insult. It had been over two years since the last attempt, and that, like all the others, had ended in failure and death. I think he really believed that his so-called "guests" owed him some sort of allegiance for all the generous hospitality, the food and lodging, the drugs and entertainment he lavished upon them, not to mention the sheer honor of knowing him. He regarded escape attempts as a form of treason and, worse yet, bad manners.

Dismissing me with a grunt, Ching Wei waved at his guards to take me away. As I left, I heard him barking urgent orders into a microphone on his electronic console.

It took them less than a week to track down those kids. Predictably, they'd run due south into the mountains, sticking to the high ridges and avoiding the well-trodden trails that ran through the valleys. But Lopper's trackers picked up the scent as easily as bloodhounds. A Shan or Karen hunter can smell smoke three to five miles away and tell you exactly what's burning and where it's coming from. So they simply followed the trail of smoldering campfires and garbage which they so carelessly left in their wake. Survival training in the Rockies didn't do them much good in Burma.

    Only three came back alive. Laura had tried to make a run for it and was shot dead in her tracks and left to rot in the jungle. Tom, with his curly red hair and long walrus moustache, had his head taken off as a trophy for Lopper, and his corpse too was dumped along the trail. Blond Vicki was specifically saved as a gift for Captain Lu, the officer who'd kidnapped the group. He abused her so badly that she killed herself within a month by eating an overdose of raw opium. The other two were paraded naked through the village, then trussed up like chickens and slowly boiled to death in the cauldron in Ching Wei's courtyard.

    Their screams rang clearly across the valley and echoed all the way up to where I lay smoking with Moreau.

XXI

When Carter announced on December 16, 1978, that America had decided to grant formal diplomatic recognition to the communist regime in China, Ching Wei erupted in a ranting rage of righteous indignation. "How dare they!" he fumed. "After all these years that we have fought together for the cause of freedom!" He'd always idealized America as the world's greatest bastion of freedom and anticommunist resistance, and he loathed Carter for what he perceived to be the ultimate political betrayal of the century. The fact that Carter hadn't even bothered to forewarn the Nationalist Chinese government in Taiwan of his intention to cut them loose and deal instead with the enemy in Peking further offended Ching Wei, and he expressed his outrage by abruptly ordering the immediate execution of six Americans.

Had Ching Wei exercised his usual discretion in selecting victims for slaughter, things might have gone differently for him in the end. But this time, in his blind fury over Carter's decision to establish diplomatic relations with Communist China, he simply barked a command at his chief bodyguard—a sadistic brute named Lai—to round up half a dozen Americans for immediate execution. He sweetened the job for Lai by also granting him the role of executioner.

Lai trotted a brigade of Black Dragons straight down to Poong and grabbed the first six Americans he found wandering in and around the village. One of them turned out to be Reeves, one of the American POWs Weasel had liberated from that prison camp in Laos a while back. Reeves had the misfortune to be sitting under a bodhi tree near the shop, reading a newspaper, when Lai's hunting party pounced on him and dragged him away. Since his arrival at Dragon Mountain, Reeves had become a very close friend of Lopper's, so close that there had been some talk of Reeves moving up to live next door to Lopper in the Lurp village.

Had Lopper been around when Lai and his goons nabbed Reeves, he might have been able to intervene in time to save Reeves's neck. And had Ching Wei bothered to check who was who among the victims Lai had seized, he surely would have spared Reeves as a gesture of respect to Lopper, for Lopper was one of Ching Wei's most important and trusted allies. But in the event, Lopper and most of the Lurps were way up-country on a recon mission deep inside Wild Wa territory, and Ching Wei had worked himself up into such a towering rage against America that he was prepared to execute President Carter and his entire Cabinet, if only he could get his hands on them. No one else dared speak a word on behalf of Reeves or any of the other victims, for we all knew perfectly well that once Ching Wei had issued an order, he never took it back, and anyone who expressed sympathy or support for a condemned victim usually ended up on the chopping block with him.

As usual whenever Ching Wei wished to teach the world a lesson it would not soon forget, everyone was required to attend the execution in Poong. For starters, Ching Wei launched himself into a long, rambling diatribe against the duplicity of American foreign policy, and by extension the hypocrisy of the American people in general. He brayed a shrill litany of complaint against America, citing several historical examples of how America had betrayed China in the past, and heaping scathing scorn on *"that stupid country bumpkin, the former peanut farmer Carter."*

Hoffmann must have jacked him up with a real mean brew for the occasion, and he was spiteful as an angry snake.

Finally, he ended his tirade and signaled Lai and his hellhounds to proceed. Lai had each victim trussed naked to a stake in such a way that their bellies protruded out. He had decided to take this opportunity to show off his skill at killing a man with a single circular cut to the gut that emptied his bowels and other abdominal organs into a wicker basket on the ground, while leaving the victim's heart and lungs intact so that he stayed alive long enough to witness the gore and feel the pain. It was such a vile display of sheer cruelty that it made me feel ashamed to be a member of the human species.

After it was over and Ching Wei had left, I went over to Reeves's corpse and yanked his dog tags off his neck as a memento for Lopper, who returned a few weeks later. When Lopper heard what had happened to his good friend Reeves, he didn't say a word. He immediately packed up a month's provisions and disappeared again into the jungle, this time completely by himself. He didn't come back for over three weeks, and when he did, he still had nothing to say about what happened to Reeves. He acted as if nothing at all had happened.

Three months later, my wife, Sasha, died in San Francisco, and I felt it the moment it happened.

Ling Yun had been training me in what he called "dream wandering." First he made me give up all forms of smoking—tobacco, ganja, opium, the whole works. *"It is not the drug's effect but the smoke itself that obstructs the flow of chi through the vital channels,"* he said. He made me meditate for hours at a time, facing due south from the mouth of his cave. One day, without warning, he suddenly pounded me hard on the back a few times, just below my right shoulder blade. It felt like a sledgehammer and knocked the wind clear out of me. But when I caught my breath again, I knew that I'd been changed forever. I felt energy pulsing through my whole system like high-voltage electricity, rattling my bones and chattering my teeth. An immense "opening" sensation unfolded deep down inside my gut and all along my spine. I poured sweat and would have probably passed out, if Ling Yun hadn't come to the rescue by poking his fingers sharply into various vital energy points on my neck, chest, and legs. That calmed me down instantly, though I still felt a bit giddy and light-headed.

What Ling Yun had done was to open up the "Eight Mysterious Channels" through which the cosmic energies of the universe enter into and flow through the human energy system. These invisible arteries form a network of energy channels that Ling Yun referred to as our "spirit bodies." This web of subtle energy cannot be seen by ordinary eyesight, but accomplished spiritual adepts may easily perceive it as a luminous aura of rainbow-colored light. By freeing this spirit body from the bondage of flesh, we can project our consciousness beyond the physical body and direct it to wherever we wish to go. *"There are gateways in your mind where dreams and reality merge as one,"* Ling Yun explained. *"Your task is to go inside and find those gates, and when they open, you must seize the moment to pass through to the other side."*

After he opened up my channels, I started having incredibly lucid dreams, and Ling Yun instructed me to scrutinize the dreamscapes carefully for familiar signs. *"Try to look at the corners of your dreams,"* he suggested, *"not at the central figures. Look for patterns, not concrete details."* He taught me secret breathing exercises and eye movements to facilitate the process and told me to perform them every night before going to sleep.

I practiced diligently for about a year, but nothing noteworthy happened until one night in late February 1979. I dreamed I was standing in a vaguely familiar room, staring at a bed. On the bed lay a pale and ghostly woman draped in white. I tried to analyze the scene rationally, but drew a

Dragon Mountain

blank. Then I recalled Ling Yun's advice and looked down at the corners of the dreamscape. There I saw something so familiar that it almost jolted me awake. At first it was just an elegant geometric pattern, but something about it tugged tenaciously at my memory, and suddenly everything came into clear focus. It was the Oriental carpet on which I'd learned to crawl and walk as a baby. I'd inherited it from my father, and ever since 1950, it's been on the bedroom floor of our apartment in San Francisco. Looking up again at the figure on the bed, I now recognized her instantly: it was my wife, Sasha. I knew beyond a doubt that I—or some part of me—was standing beside her in our own bedroom back home in San Francisco. She looked terribly ill, and her loneliness was so palpable that it filled the room like a cold fog.

She looked over at me and said, "I'm dying, Jack."

I tried to move closer, but my feet seemed glued to the floor.

"I'm dying," she repeated weakly, then turned her head away and said no more. I panicked, and the dream began to dissolve. The harder I fought to hold onto it, the faster it faded away. I woke up trembling in a cold sweat.

It was nearly dawn, so I got up and went out to the garden to try and calm myself down with a round of deep breathing and stretching exercises. Soon I felt the energy radiating along my inner channels and heating up my gut, and wafts of steam rose from my shoulders and head. I focused my attention on the flow of energy and followed it through two complete cycles—from the lower gut up along the spine, over the top of the head, then down the arms and legs into the hands and feet, and back up to the genitals and gut. There it gathered itself for the next cycle.

Then suddenly my entire gut wrenched and twisted up tight as a steel spring. A rending explosion erupted inside me, blasting the air from my lungs and evacuating my bladder and bowels. I fainted. When I recovered consciousness, I found myself sprawled on the ground, gasping for breath and clutching my gut. And at that precise moment I knew with absolute certainty that Sasha had just died. The Chinese term for what we mean when we say "broken heart" came to mind *duan chang*, which literally means "broken gut." I'd often wondered why. Now I knew.

For weeks after that, I felt completely hollow, as if all my energy had drained out through a big hole in my belly. *"That's because there is a big hole in your belly,"* Ling Yun explained when I went to see him about it. *"I can see it quite clearly. When two people grow very close through love and mutual devotion, their energy auras interact and resonate together in specific patterns that are unique to that relationship, and this interaction functions even when they are physically apart. The longer the relationship continues, the stronger these living bonds of energy grow. That is why old married couples who have been together in love for many years always seem to know what their partners are thinking and feeling. Because they share precise patterns of energy unique to their relationship, whatever affects one also affects the other in exactly the same way.*

"When one partner dies, these unique patterns of energy which they shared for so long begin to dissolve in the surviving partner, leaving a big hole in the living partner's energy system, usually in the lower gut. Ordinary people are not aware of these holes, but they suffer the ill effects just the same. For adepts who have cultivated sensitivity to chi, the pain of this unraveling energy feels as sharp as a knife in the belly. Over time, these holes repair themselves, but during this time, one must be extremely careful, for such holes leave both body and spirit highly vulnerable to disease, degeneration, death, and all sorts of evil influences." He made me lie down for hours on the ground inside his cave and smeared my entire torso with a potent herbal poultice. *"This will speed the healing process and prevent excessive loss of power,"* he said, and sure enough, I soon recovered my vitality and balance.

I later mentioned this incident to Ching Wei and requested that his people in Bangkok obtain copies of the *San Francisco Chronicle* for the entire week during which my dream had occurred. Ching Wei knew about my apprenticeship with Ling Yun, and he himself had a strong interest in such esoteric phenomena, so he readily agreed.

Three months later the newspapers came in, and I shuffled through the obituary columns until I found the confirmation I was looking for:

> Sasha Robertson, 54, died
> peacefully in her sleep at home,
> after a prolonged illness. She
> is survived by her two sons,
> Duncan and Frank, and her
> mother Anna.

There was no mention of me as her surviving husband. As far as the world was concerned, I too was dead and gone.

XXII

In May, Dr. Hoffmann invited me up to his bungalow for lunch, then took me into his lab and locked the door behind us.

"I've done it!" he blurted, clapping me so hard on the back that I almost slipped into a trance. "A few final adjustments, and the formula is mine!"

"What the hell are you talking about?" So much had happened since Hoffmann first revealed his scheme to me that I'd completely forgotten about it.

"The formula, Dummkopf! The formula for China White! Our passport to freedom! I have finally discovered the secret." He paced furiously around the lab, barely able to contain his excitement. "A few final adjustments and the formula is mine," he repeated.

"You really think he'll go for it?" I asked, after he'd refreshed my memory about his plan to squeeze Ching Wei for a million bucks and safe passage home to Switzerland in exchange for the formula for China White. I'd stopped thinking about leaving Dragon Mountain long ago, and felt no motivation to do so. What the hell did I have to go back to?

"Ach, Jack," Hoffmann muttered impatiently, "lately you have become like a man living in a dream. Of course, he will go for it! Ching Wei would give both his testicles for that formula. With it he would become the undisputed drug lord of the world. It would revolutionize the narcotics trade just as ordinary heroin did when it first came onto the market. Even more important, it would free him of his dependence on China. Yes, he will agree."

"But what makes you so sure he'd let me fly out of here with you? After all, I'm his personal pilot. He might make you walk to Thailand."

"Gott im Himmel, Jack! To him you are but a convenience, an amusement. He could kidnap a dozen pilots like you if he wished. And furthermore, he now has excellent replacements for you among those American POWs brought here from Laos. Nothing, nothing is more important to him than this formula, least of all you!"

He had a point. All these years I'd served not only as Ching Wei's pilot, but also as a sounding board for his strange ideas and grandiose schemes, and as a foil for his stupid jokes. He liked having me around because I spoke Chinese and could discuss Taoist alchemy, martial arts, and other aspects of traditional Chinese culture with him. His own minions couldn't care less about these things, and his other white guests could barely use chopsticks, much less speak Chinese. I was certainly a convenience and an amusement to him, but in no way a necessity.

I had one last reservation, but Hoffmann had anticipated that. "You can stop worrying about your son in Taipei. His safety will, of course, be guaranteed as part of my bargain with Ching Wei. He will have no reason to harm your son if he permits you to leave with me."

"All right," I told Hoffmann, "I'll go along with it, but only if we're clear on one point: this whole scheme is your idea, and I'm just an innocent bystander. If he agrees to pay you off and let me fly you out of here in exchange for the formula, I'll do it. But if it backfires on you, you're on your own. I knew nothing about it. Agreed?"

"Agreed! Just leave everything to me."

"Meanwhile, I still think you're nuts."

"Nuts? Nusse? What have nuts to do with this?"

The decade closed on a sour note for Ching Wei, and as usual, his worst luck came at Chinese New Year. Shortly after Christmas in 1979, Thai Rangers attacked and destroyed Ching Wei's newly established base on the Thai-Burma border 250 miles south of Dragon Mountain. Worse yet, Ching Wei was there when it happened and had not been forewarned. He barely escaped with his life.

He'd gone down there to oversee the final stages of decoration in a lavish villa he'd constructed for himself and to install a few of his favorite concubines there. He'd been in residence for about two weeks when the Rangers stormed the place.

There must have been another big shakeup in Bangkok for the Thais to hit him so hard, especially without the usual courtesy of a forewarning. This time they were definitely playing for keeps. Eight hundred Rangers came in at night, armed with machine guns, grenade launchers, and recoilless rifles. They surrounded the entire camp; then a fat colonel approached the main barracks and shouted through a megaphone.

"I hereby place you all under arrest in the name of the Royal Government of Thailand! You are charged with smuggling narcotics, illegal possession of firearms, and subversive activities. Throw down your weapons and surrender immediately!"

A few men stumbled out of the barracks, weapons in hand, to see what the commotion was about. The moment they stepped outside, spotlights caught them in a flood of bright light. They'd been drinking beer and smoking ganja all night, and at first they must have thought the intrusion was some sort of joke.

"Throw down your weapons!" the officer barked again. Clearly, this was no joke. But instead of complying with the officer's command, the idiots raised their guns and started firing blindly into the night. A hail of bullets cut them down. The rest of the men came pouring out through the windows and doors like mad hornets with their guns blazing, and the battle was on.

Ching Wei had about five hundred men defending the new camp, but the Rangers outnumbered them and were also better armed. The Thais didn't bother to coordinate the raid with Burmese military authorities in Rangoon, and therefore Ching

Wei's avenue of escape across the Burma border remained wide open to him and strictly off-limits to the Thais. In the darkness and confusion of the initial firefight, Ching Wei's bodyguards managed to whisk him out of the besieged encampment through an underground tunnel, and he escaped unscathed across the border into Burma.

Ching Wei ordered his troops to stay behind and fight it out with the Rangers, no doubt to cover his own escape. Due to their fierce resistance, the Rangers assumed that Ching Wei was trapped inside the camp, and so the battle raged back and forth for nearly three days. They took the camp only after calling in heavy air support, but they still had to fight their way in from tree to tree, hut to hut. On the third night, the remnants of Ching Wei's troops conceded the battle and hightailed it back to Burma. They left behind over one hundred dead, but they evacuated all of their wounded. Later, I read in the *Bangkok Post* that the Thais lost forty-five killed and sixty wounded in the operation. According to the report in the newspaper, "The Rangers destroyed the elusive opium warlord's last major base on Thai territory, although they failed to net the culprit."

The loss of this camp enraged Ching Wei. He had fortified it at great expense and had just finished equipping his personal villa there with all sorts of extravagant luxuries, including a movie theater, highly sophisticated communications systems, a bowling alley, and a large swimming pool lined with tiles of Burmese jade. In another story headlined "Rangers Route Opium Kingpin from Jungle Palace," the *Bangkok Post* made a big deal over all this opulence, describing in great detail the tennis courts, air-conditioned barracks, satellite dishes, foreign provisions, and other luxuries enjoyed by Ching Wei's troops there.

Ching Wei knew there was a standing reward for any information leading to his capture, and he suspected the villagers on the Thai side of the border of informing on him. How else would the Thai command know that he was there that night? A maid or gardener or coolie conscripted from the village must have informed the Thai authorities. He'd had considerable trouble bending the elders of this village to his will when he first moved into the area, and they deeply resented being forced to supply labor and materials to construct his camp, especially while Ching Wei's own men sat around all day chewing betel and playing cards. Unlike the simple Shan folk at Dragon Mountain, who enjoyed their symbiotic relationship with Ching Wei, Thai peasants were not impressed with his lavish gifts, nor did his decadent habits sit well with their devout Buddhist beliefs.

As usual, Ching Wei insisted on exacting his revenge. He subtracted the forty-five Rangers his men had killed from the one hundred seven he'd lost and concluded that the Thais owed him sixty-two lives. He waited until the village was entirely back to normal, then sent down 300 heavily armed troops in broad daylight to exact retribution. They plundered the entire village, including the temple, of all its gold, jewels, and cash, then torched it and shot to death sixty-two villagers, including the chief and his two sons.

The Thai government responded by raising the reward for Ching Wei's head to $250,000, a price tag that offended him as being far too low.

A major consequence of the Ranger raid on Ching Wei's last outpost in Thailand was to transform him from the "Opium King" of the Golden Triangle into the "Heroin King." With both of his Thai bases knocked out and further collusion with Thai officials no longer possible, Ching Wei had no place to transport his enormous stockpiles of raw opium to outside buyers. So instead, he built three new labs and went into full-scale heroin production.

Heroin is far more compact than opium and therefore much easier to pack and conceal, and a lot easier to transport undetected. It's also far more profitable. The only drawback was the bad publicity, but Ching Wei no longer seemed to care about that. He now sent his couriers all the way down to Bangkok, Hong Kong, Penang, and beyond to market the stuff directly, and he bribed enough customs officers along the way to reduce his risks and losses to a minimum. By the summer of 1980, Ching Wei was making more money than ever.

XXIII

After my astral visit to my wife's deathbed in San Francisco, Ling Yun accelerated my training program. On several occasions he sent me spinning into space on terrifying journeys, simply by pressing his forefingers firmly against vital points on my temples. Whenever he did that, a flash of white light erupted in my mind, sending my consciousness hurdling through an invisible gate. Then I'd find myself floating freely as a wreath of smoke, fully aware of everything around me, but devoid of all physical sensations.

Eventually I mastered the technique called "stepping out of the flesh." He instructed me to build a kind of wooden crib in which to sit while meditating. It was shaped like a little boat or bathtub, constructed in such a way that I could sit comfortably inside, with my back and head supported and my knees drawn up in a fetal position. After performing the requisite breathing exercises and eye movements, I was supposed to sit in the crib and meditate on a single thought or image, while completely relaxing every fiber of my body and letting my mind drift slowly into blank reverie. First there came a deep trance—dark, still, silent, yet not quite like sleep. At this stage, the slightest stray thought or random emotion would instantly break the spell, and I'd either wake up with a jolt or fall into a deep sleep.

But when I succeeded in maintaining an undisturbed trance long enough for the Eight Mysterious Channels to open, cosmic energy would pour into my system through the crown of my head like a torrential waterfall, causing my entire body to shake, rattle, and roll. The purpose of the crib, Ling Yun said, was to prevent me from rolling all over the place and injuring myself.

The final step is to "tame the wind" with proper breathing, fine tuning it until the incoming power synchronizes with one's own energy pulses. Gradually the thunderous roar becomes a smooth purring hum, and that's the signal that you're ready to lift off into space.

That's all there is to it. When you've achieved that gentle rhythmic hum, it allows you to shift awareness and volition from the physical body over to the astral energy body, and you can then go anywhere you wish with it. To "lift off," you simply will your astral energy body to rise free of your flesh. Next thing you know, you're floating in the air. Look down and you see your own body lying sound asleep beneath you. The first time I did it, the sight of my own body lying separated from my self gave me such a shock that I snapped back into my flesh with a terrible jolt and woke up vomiting.

It's impossible to describe in words how odd that state of being feels, but I assure you that it's every bit as real as the normal state, if not more so. Things appear visible by virtue of their own inner glow rather than the reflected light we perceive through normal physical vision. If you focus on any particular object for too long, it either melts away or changes shape. The easiest time to enter that dimension is late at night, especially between 3:00 AM and dawn. *"Unlike the body,"* Ling Yun told me, *"the spirit sees best at night."*

I was floating pleasantly over the little crib in my room late one night, when suddenly I rose up through the ceiling and rocketed into the sky, accelerating so fast that everything became a fleeting blur. It literally felt like "soaring in the clouds," a feeling of perfect freedom and mobility. Now I knew why Ling Yun had devoted his life to these arts, for nothing on earth compares to the sheer bliss of shedding the flesh and letting the spirit roam free, while remaining alive and fully aware of it all.

I could have soared through space forever, it felt so good, but after a while, I started dropping gently through the clouds like a snowflake drifting to the ground. A city appeared below, and I scanned it for clues that might identify it in my mind. I noticed a familiar checkerboard pattern formed by the clay-tiled roofs of square, squat houses neatly set in rows bordered by narrow, Oriental lanes, and suddenly I recognized the memory: I knew without a doubt that I was hovering over the city of Taipei. I'd flown in and out of that city for ten years prior to my transfer to Saigon, and those checkerboard patterns had appeared before my eyes hundreds of times as I banked over the city to land at the airport.

I descended slowly through the roof of an old Chinese house near Round Hill Park and found myself floating inside a cluttered room. My attention was drawn instinctively to a figure sleeping on a bed. Moving a bit closer, I saw that it was my old teacher, Master Lee. He felt my presence and began to stir. Gradually the upper part of his astral energy body emerged and sat up in bed, but the lower half remained fused in flesh.

He gazed at me, and his aura grew brighter, then I felt him say, *"Luo Bao-shan, so it's you."* There was no hint of surprise in his reaction, which came to me as a flickering beam of light that I received and interpreted somewhere deep in the center of my gut.

I beamed back my delight at finding him there and mentioned Ling Yun. Instantly, Ling Yun's form appeared as a web of soft light hovering in the room, throbbing red and orange with joy. Rays of light flashed back and forth between Ling Yun and Old Lee, and while I couldn't follow their exchange intelligibly, I could clearly feel their happiness. Then Ling Yun's form faded away and disappeared as abruptly as it had come.

"Ling Yun tells me that you have made great progress," Old Lee beamed at me. *"You must continue to practice and pay close attention to what Master Ling teaches you."* Then he transmitted the amazing information that my son Duncan had wandered into his tai

chi class at Round Hill Park one morning and had taken up martial arts training under his tutelage, just as I had done years ago in Chungking during the war. Old Lee had recognized Duncan the same way Ching Wei had identified him in the bar—by his Chinese name, Luo Bao-shan. It was the name Old Lee himself had given me when I became his student in Chungking. My son had adopted the same name after moving to Taiwan to study Chinese. Old Lee said that he had become one of his best students, just as I had done back in China, and that made me feel so happy that I almost jetted off into space.

Old Lee did not seem able to muster sufficient volition and vitality to draw himself completely out of his physical body. Life in the big city had taken its toll on his power. So he sat there halfway emerged, and we continued to beam messages at each other for a while. Soon his energy began to fade, and his aura grew dim. As he sank slowly back into his slumbering body, I beamed him farewell and soared up through the roof and into the clouds, flying fast and free through space.

I must have tracked the Tropic of Cancer all the way around the planet on my way back to Dragon Mountain. I had distinct impressions of islands and oceans, mountains and cities flashing by swiftly below. Time meant nothing. I found that I could slow down or speed up my flight by a simple exertion of will, and that I could intuitively identify almost anything that caught my attention. Somewhere over Mexico, I sensed a strong, very dense patch of hot human energy pulsating from a spot on the ground, throbbing and glowing like a bonfire. When I focused attention on it, I saw in a flash that it was a bullfight, and that the entire crowd of thousands of spectators was resonating as one living entity with the matador, as he faced down a very angry bull.

I zoomed back to Dragon Mountain and found myself floating over my own body again, surrounded by the familiar surroundings of my own room at Moreau's. I looked down, and there I saw myself hunched in the little crib, hands folded over my stomach, legs splayed out to make room for a throbbing erection. The instinctive embarrassment I felt at seeing myself in that condition broke the trance abruptly, and I snapped back into my body like a stretched rubber band released. I woke up with a terrible ache in my gut, sweating and thoroughly exhausted.

I reported my experience to Ling Yun, and he was very pleased. He mentioned his own brief appearance at Old Lee's side and said that he'd bowed out early in order not to interfere with the frequencies of energy I was exchanging with Old Lee. When I told him of the embarrassing sight that caused me to snap together again prematurely, he laughed uproariously. *"That is perfectly natural and no cause for embarrassment,"* he said. *"You should be more ashamed of the other uses to which you have applied your Yang tool over the years. Sexual energy is the fundamental fuel that permits the spirit to separate from the flesh and soar free on wings of pure power. Have you not noticed that when you awaken—even from ordinary dreams—your Yang tool is hard? We possess no more potent source of energy than that which is stored in our genitals. It is the very essence of life. Even at my age, whenever I go soaring in the clouds, my Jade Stalk stands at full attention until I return to my body. Without the sexual force, we could never break through the bonds of flesh to explore the universe. That is why it is so important for adepts of the Mysterious Arts to conserve their sexual vitality. Without it, we are like wingless birds."*

Ling Yun warned me to land more carefully next time. *"It is most important to bring the spirit and flesh together again slowly and gently."* He gave me one of his herbal concoctions and massaged my lower abdomen with his palms. Immediately, I felt his energy radiating into my system, restoring my equilibrium, and banishing the giddy feeling that had lingered inside me.

"You have found the gateless gate between the worlds, and last night you passed freely through it on your own power," he told me. *"You have no more need now for talk about these matters. You have directly experienced the ultimate nature of reality and entered realms of eternity unknown to ordinary mortals. Your task now is to cultivate the truth that transcends all words and to live strictly by that truth in every single thing you do, say, and think. Only then shall you become a True Man of Tao. Henceforth, only your own inner light can illuminate your way. If you attempt to grasp these things with reason, you will lose everything!"*

XXIV

Lopper finally made his move at Ching Wei's annual Chinese New Year's Eve party on February 4, 1981. It had been nearly two years since Ching Wei had ordered the slaughter of those six Americans, including Lopper's good friend Reeves, as a personal protest against America's political rapprochement with Communist China. All this time Lopper had been silently nursing his grudge, waiting for the right moment to act, and he found that moment at the stroke of midnight on the eve of the Year of the Rooster.

It started out as a great party. As usual on the auspicious occasion of Chinese New Year, Ching Wei refrained from staging the bloody displays of torture and death that marked most of his parties. Instead he opted for more conventional forms of entertainment that night: an acrobatic show, a couple of clever magicians, an amateur striptease performed by some of his palace maids, and, of course, the requisite fanfare of fireworks at midnight. Ironically, even though he usually showed his best face at this time of year, it was always at Chinese New Year that his luck ran worst, and this year it ran out completely.

All of his senior Chinese officers were there, seated at one end of the banquet table, while a selection of his favorite "foreign guests," including all the Lurps, and a few local village elders sat at the other end, with Ching Wei perched in the middle. Due to the seniority I'd gained there after more than nine years, plus my ability to speak fluent Chinese, I was seated on Ching Wei's immediate left.

He'd arranged a particularly spectacular fireworks show this year, brought over at great expense all the way from Taiwan, and therefore the banquet table was set outside in the courtyard, where we could all enjoy the pyrotechnics from our own chairs, without interrupting the flow of food, drink, and conversation. Other than the invited guests seated at the table, the only people allowed in the palace compound were Ching Wei's personal female retinue of maids, concubines, and dancers, and his brigade of bloodthirsty bodyguards, the Black Dragons, who patrolled the grounds continuously throughout the evening, like a pack of trained guard dogs.

A few minutes before midnight, Lopper stood up from the table and excused himself to go to the toilet. Hunch followed a minute later, lurching into the shadows as though he were drunk. No one even noticed, except me. Just as the first sky rocket crumped and lit up the firmament, Katz and Teach slipped away from the table too, but everyone's eyes were riveted on the dazzling display in the sky, and again no one but me noticed. I'd been picking up strange signals in my gut all evening from Lopper's energy—a swelling sense of foreboding—so I paid him close attention that night.

The pyrotechnic extravaganza lasted about ten to twelve minutes. Toward the end of the show, had anyone been listening carefully, he would surely have heard a few unusually short, sharp claps detonate nearby, mixed in with the staccato clatter of firecrackers from beyond the wall. But no one noticed that either, except me.

As the glitter from the last sky rocket fizzled away and the echo of the final firecracker faded off into the hills, something else immediately caught everyone's attention, something no one failed to notice. An intensely bright red dot danced like a dervish back and forth across the table, leaping from one end to the other, then came to rest on Ching Wei's crystal goblet, casting crimson rays of refracted light all over the place. At that moment, everyone suddenly noticed that the Lurps were missing from the table, and in the same instant we all realized that we were looking at a laser beam, the kind mounted on high-caliber rifles to pinpoint targets. Before anyone could say a word, a shot rang out and the crystal goblet exploded, scattering wine and shards of glass onto Ching Wei's lap. The little red dot crawled slowly to the edge of the table, crept up Ching Wei's robe, and stopped dead center on his heart. Katz was out there somewhere, letting Ching Wei know that he had him pegged in his sights.

It was a very dramatic moment. An eerie calm settled over the table, but it felt ripe with doom, as though a live grenade were rolling loose under the table and everyone knew it. All eyes stayed glued on the bright red dot at Ching Wei's heart, waiting for it to explode again.

Then Lopper stepped quietly out of the shadows. In one hand he held a big bloody bowie knife; in the other he clutched the freshly severed head of Lai, Ching Wei's chief bodyguard and commander of the dreaded Black Dragons. He held Lai's head by its long braided queue, letting it swing by his side like a satchel as he slowly approached the table. All the while, the laser beam remained riveted at the center of Ching Wei's chest.

Lopper stepped up to the middle of the table and stood directly across from Ching Wei. He raised Lai's head up to eye level and gave it a spin with the tip of his bowie knife, sending droplets of blood twirling onto the tablecloth. Gazing intently at Lai's head as though inspecting a newly acquired work of art, he muttered, "I've had a shelf on a big old oak waiting for you nearly two years now." Then he set Lai's head down on the table right in front of Ching Wei, facing him, and said, "The others are all dead." Lai's head stared balefully at Ching Wei, lips frozen in a mute snarl. A collar of blood oozed thickly from his severed neck and pooled on the table. No one said a word.

It was the perfect palace coup, executed with flawless timing and precision. Obviously, the Lurps couldn't come to Ching Wei's New Year's Eve party carrying guns, so instead they'd sawed down a few Wild Wa blowguns to about ten inches and tucked them inside the legs of their pants, loaded with darts dipped in deadly Wa nerve toxin. They'd killed the first few guards quickly at close range with the blowguns, then used the guards' own weapons to shoot the rest of them, while the fireworks still provided cover for the sound of gunfire. By the time the last firecracker popped, the job was done, and the Black Dragons were dead ducks.

I think everyone at the table knew immediately what this was all about—everyone except Ching Wei, who looked surprised and extremely annoyed. Lopper had just beheaded his chief bodyguard, and killed all the others as well, in the presence of his senior officers and foreign guests. Worse yet, he'd had the audacity to do it on the auspicious occasion of Chinese New Year. If Ching Wei somehow managed to get out of this alive, he'd have to kill Lopper and all the Lurps in order to restore face and retain his authority over his men, and Lopper knew that. By the same token, if Lopper ever wished to sleep in peace again, without the constant specter of Ching Wei's vendetta haunting him, he'd have to kill Ching Wei, and Ching Wei knew that too. You could almost taste the bitterness brewing between them.

"*Insolent pye-dog!*" Ching Wei howled at Lopper. "*Shameless spawn of a filthy tortoise!* How dare you disturb my New Year festivities! What is the meaning of this rude disruption, this shameless abuse of my friendship and hospitality?"

"Tell him, Jack," Lopper snarled. "Tell him in his own lingo what this is all about. Tell him how I feel about this pig Lai carving up my pal Reeves. Talk about rude! Talk about abuse of friendship!" He stood there glowering at Ching Wei, two years of righteous indignation simmering inside.

So I told him in Chinese. I told him how he let Lai butcher Lopper's good friend Reeves in that execution he staged two years ago, while Lopper was slogging up-country on a dangerous mission for him. I recalled how careful he used to be about selecting victims for slaughter, so that no one need live in fear of an unjust death at Dragon Mountain, and I reminded him how important personal friendship was for the Lurps, and for all of us, after all these years in the jungle. "*The bond of friendship is especially important to Lopper,*" I pointed out. "*He relies upon it entirely to cultivate the personal loyalty that serves as a basis for his leadership. He is not just another uncivilized barbarian, like most Americans. He has learned much here in Asia. He understands the central importance of righteousness, propriety, and justice in the conduct of human affairs.*" The Chinese mind always responds well to a lofty philosophical pitch, so I laid it on thick. "*Had he failed to avenge the wrongful death of his heart-friend by killing Lai, he would have lost the loyalty and respect of all his compatriots, and the shame would have weighed on his heart like a stone forever after. You truly should have been more careful whose guts you let Lai spill that day.*"

As I spoke, the expression of annoyed surprise on Ching Wei's face gradually softened. A fleeting look of exasperation arose, as though he felt galled by his own misstep, but it passed swiftly, and by the time I'd finished speaking, he looked completely calm and self-composed again.

Ching Wei was no fool. He knew that Lopper was a man of honor—indeed, that was the quality he most admired in him. He also realized that he had violated Lopper's honor by carelessly having his friend killed—needlessly and without the slightest provocation. This would never have happened had he not made the inexcusable blunder of allowing an external event that had nothing whatsoever to do with his own internal affairs to cloud his mind with such anger and passion that he failed entirely to exercise his usual care and discretion in handling these matters. He had no one but himself to blame for that oversight. Moreover, had he wished to make a political statement by killing a few Americans, he could easily have taken his pick from the many useless louts and derelicts there, none of whom would have been missed by anyone. Ching Wei had blown it, and he knew it. And the blunder would cost him his kingdom.

He pursed his lips in a wry pout and heaved a sigh. Then he smiled. Snapping his fingers at a maid who cowered nearby, he commanded her to bring him a new goblet and told to her to refill everyone's glass with wine. She was so nervous that she had to grip the bottle with both hands to control her trembling. When everyone's drink had been replenished, Ching Wei stood up and raised his glass from the table.

First he addressed Lopper. "I'm sorry about your friend," he said evenly, not a trace of tension in his voice. "It was a careless mistake, but unfortunately it cannot be corrected. You have done what you must do." Then he turned to his senior officers and spoke in Chinese. "*'Spilled water can never be collected again.' I spilled his friend's blood without cause, and the consequences belong to me alone. The time has come for me to retire from the stage and take my leave. You have all served me well. I enjoin you to serve your new commander equally well.*" Then he swung his goblet around the table and addressed everyone. "Let us all drink one last toast together, to welcome the Year of the Golden Rooster. Thank you all for your excellent company here at Dragon Mountain. May you all enjoy good health, great happiness, and abundant prosperity in the New Year." As he raised his glass to his lips, he shot me a sidelong glance and said, "To old times, Captain Jack," exactly the same words he'd used to toast me on my first night there nine years ago. "Everybody together now: bottoms up!" He tossed back his head and drained the glass dry, and we all followed suit. Slamming the empty glass back down on the table, he snapped a formal military salute at Lopper and sat down again.

The rest happened so fast that no one saw it but me, and even I didn't realize what he was doing until it was done. Settling himself back into his chair beside me, he casually clasped his hands in his lap. The next moment, a bright green glint flashed briefly from his fingers, catching my eye and drawing my attention down to his lap. It came from the glittering emerald embedded in the tip of his jewel-encrusted fingernail sheath, which he was slowly pulling off the little finger of his left hand. Never in the nine years I'd been there had I ever seen him take it off. The nail was at least two inches long, slightly curved and filed down to a sharp point. As the tip of the nail emerged from the sheath, I saw an oily drop of dark green fluid clinging to the sharpened point. Before I could register what I was seeing, he folded the first three fingers against his palm and locked them in place with his thumb, then pointed the long nail up toward his face. It rose from his lap like a rocket, as he drove it with unerring accuracy into the inner corner of his left eye, sinking it in to the hilt.

For a few seconds he just sat there, stiff and straight as a pillar, fingernail buried in his eye. Then a tremendous shudder shook his spine and jerked his head. Both arms and both legs shot out straight in front of him, and blood gushed from the wound in his eye. His head jerked once more, then he collapsed face down on the table, arms spread and legs splayed, and lay there still as stone.

No one made a sound. All eyes locked on Ching Wei. A few of us still held our empty glasses aloft, hands frozen in midair from the toast we'd just drunk with him. It seemed like everyone was holding his breath, waiting to see if this were all for real, or just another one of his clever jokes.

Lopper finally broke the silence with a loud cluck of his tongue. "Now that was a real class act," he drawled softly. "I didn't think he had the spunk for that."

"Nerve toxin, I'd say," said Teach. "Probably the same Wa stuff we used to bag his bodyguards. Works instantly. Never fails. Good choice."

No one had anything to add to that, and another long silence fell over the table. Hoffmann looked crestfallen: there went his ticket home and his million-dollar retirement plan. Now Lopper was king of the mountain, and he wouldn't give a fig for Hoffmann's formula. Or would he?

Ching Wei's blood seeped out around his head and puddled together with Lai's, then crept slowly across the table and dribbled over the edge. It had all happened in the blink of the eye: a moment ago, Ching Wei was standing there wishing us all a happy new year; now he lay slabbed out on the table, dead as a dodo. Our minds were still digesting what our eyes had just seen, when Lopper's voice cut through the silence again. His tone was firm but friendly, like someone who wished to be obeyed but not feared.

"Translate what I say, Jack, word for word." Turning to face the Chinese officers, he pointed the tip of his knife at Lai and began his speech. "I killed Lai because Lai killed my friend Reeves without cause, and that's what happens to people who murder my friends. But I didn't kill the Boss: he died by his own hand." That was a nice touch, so I gave it a bit more spin in Chinese by saying, *He died by his own hand, and his hand was moved by Heaven."*

Lopper continued, "We've all worked together here for a long time now. This is our world, a world we've created ourselves, and life is good here for all of us, a whole lot better than it is out there. But I believe we can make it even better here than it was before, if we all stick together and no one gets too big for his breeches. Anyone who doesn't like it can get up and walk away right now." He waved his knife toward the gate, but no one moved.

"First, as my New Year gift to you and to all the troops, everyone gets a twenty percent raise in pay, across the board, effective immediately. Second, there'll be no more of those blood-and-guts killing shows. From now on, if someone needs to get executed, we do it quick and clean with a bullet to the back of the head. Third, we stop kidnapping people. We've got more than enough white folk around here now. If any more honkies move into the neighborhood, I'm moving out!" That raised a few chuckles of polite laughter around the table. Already I could feel them warming to Lopper's style of leadership.

"Tomorrow's Chinese New Year, the biggest day of the year around here. First thing in the morning, at nine o'clock sharp, I want you to assemble all the troops down in the village so that I can give them the usual New Year pep talk. Then we'll come back here and throw the usual New Year shindig for all the sawbwas and other local big shots, and we'll all be off to a great new start together." He called for the maid to pour out another round of wine. "From now on, I'm in command here, but I can't keep this place going without your help. So here's my pledge: you keep faith with me and follow my way, and I promise to provide you protection, prosperity, and professional conduct in all matters. Give me your trust, and I will honor it always." Then he raised his glass and hollered, "Cheers and cock-a-doodle-doo to you all!

Here's to a Happy Year of the Cock!" And we all tossed down another round together.

It was a command performance, and it left them all cheering and clapping. To drive home the point in terms that went to the very heart of the Chinese spirit, I capped Lopper's speech with a classical clincher. *"The Mandate of Heaven has shifted. What happened here tonight was decreed by destiny. A new leader has been chosen."* Signaling the maid to refill our glasses again, I said, *"Let us now drink a toast to congratulate the new chief and wish him a happy New Year. 'Long may he live; may he live ten thousand years!'"*

They took the cue and all stood up together. Saluting him with one hand, they raised their glasses to Lopper with the other and shouted, *"'Long may he live; may he live ten thousand years!'"* And we all drained our glasses again.

I could see that Lopper would have no trouble consolidating his coup and establishing his leadership there. For one thing, no one would miss Lai and his bloody brigade of cutthroats, and Lopper knew this from the beginning. There'd been a longstanding professional rivalry between the Lurps and the Black Dragons, and particularly between Lopper and Lai, who'd always felt bitterly jealous of the respect and honors Ching Wei accorded Lopper. Lopper always got all the glory for his daring exploits in the field, while Lai got treated more like a trained attack dog than a trusted ally. While the Lurps lived in luxury in their own village and worked only a few months each year, the Dragons had been housed in stone bunkers near the palace gates and were always at Ching Wei's beck and call, twenty-four hours a day, seven days a week.

Now, with Lai and the rest of his crew out of the way, Lopper and the Lurps had no serious rivals or enemies to contend with at Dragon Mountain. Ching Wei's Chinese officers came from a much finer cut of China's social fabric than Lai and his goons. They were professional military officers, not jealous palace guards, and most of them came from good families and were well educated. They'd worked side by side with the Lurps on many missions and admired them for their courage and cunning in the field. They'd developed particular respect for Lopper's military genius and for his strict personal code of honor. As they saw it, Lopper had put his life on the line to avenge the unjust death of a friend and fellow warrior, and they respected him all the more for that. It made them want to be his friend and fellow warrior too. Lopper had already become a legend around there long ago; now they'd witnessed him wrest the Mandate of Heaven to rule Dragon Mountain from Ching Wei's hands. It was all very Chinese, the stuff of legends, and it instantly bonded them with Lopper, who'd played his role to perfection. Furthermore, most of Ching Wei's Chinese officers were my age, a lot older than the Lurps, and they were quite content to have strong young blood take command.

Lopper's speech, and all the toasts that went with it, took the tension out of the air, and everyone finally relaxed again. I told the maid to bring another tablecloth and draped it over Lai and Ching Wei. Soon the table was buzzing with small talk, and the party continued as though nothing unusual had happened. Asians have an amazing ability to adapt instantly to sudden shifts in circumstances, quickly trimming their sails to catch the new prevailing winds. But all the drama left me feeling rattled and drained. What I needed now was not another drink but a few pipes of good opium with Moreau. I knew he usually stayed up late on special holidays, smoking his best stuff, and I wanted to get back to his place before he drifted off to dreamland, so I took Lopper aside and asked leave to go home.

"Sure," he said, escorting me to the gate to let me out. "And thanks for translating my speech for me. I don't know how you put it to them in Chinese, but it sure did the trick. Just goes to show: words are more effective than bullets, if you know how to use them."

Lai's decapitated body lay in a heap by the gate, where he'd been standing sentry when Lopper lopped off his head. We had to skirt around him to avoid stepping in the pool of gummy blood that was still oozing from his neck. "In case you're wondering," Lopper told me, "I won't be taking Ching Wei's head for my collection. We'll give him a big fancy funeral, Chinese style, with full military honors." That was the first time I ever heard Lopper refer to Ching Wei by name, rather than as "the Chink." Ching Wei's poise and bravado in the face of death had finally earned him Lopper's respect. I felt relieved to hear that Ching Wei would be buried in one piece, with his head intact upon his shoulders. To the Chinese, nothing is worse than dying with your head cut off, for it means you must cross over into the spirit world without your mental faculties—deaf, dumb, blind, and unable to enjoy the delights of Heaven.

I was even more relieved to find Moreau awake and still smoking his pipe when I got home a few minutes later.

XXV

The next morning Lopper addressed the rank and file of Ching Wei's army, who didn't hear about the previous night's events until their officers came down from the palace shortly after dawn to brief them and to muster the troops into the village square for Lopper's New Year message. Lopper kept his speech brief and cordial. When he announced the 20 percent hike in pay, the entire congregation erupted in a long, loud peal of cheers and applause. At the end of Lopper's speech, all the troops joined their officers in a resounding shout of support, *"Long may he live; may he live ten thousand years!"*

Afterward, we went back to the palace, where Lopper installed himself on Ching Wei's throne to receive traditional New Year greetings and gifts from all the village sawbwas, Chinese officers, and other local dignitaries from around the domain. Perched on his own little throne next to Lopper sat his young protégé, the Prince of Laos, beautifully attired in the elaborate silk garments of Lao royalty. His elegant style and graceful manners charmed everyone. Lopper assigned him the role of handing out the little red envelopes stuffed with lucky money to all the guests in the reception line as they passed to offer their New Year greetings.

Lopper had dressed himself in the full formal regalia of a traditional Shan chieftain before ascending the throne. He'd done his homework: all the requisite insignia and traditional emblems of Shan nobility were there, each in its proper place, and these made a deep and powerful impression on the sawbwas and other local Shan luminaries who came to pay him their New Year respects. Lopper also spoke sufficient Shan to chat with them in their own language—something that Ching Wei had never done—and this pleased them immensely. Lopper treated them all with equal respect, in complete accordance with traditional Shan protocol, and by the end of the day, he had completely won their allegiance.

Later that afternoon, after all the ritual formalities were done and everyone was busy gorging themselves at the bar and buffet tables, Lopper and I strolled through the garden and sat in the Chinese pavilion by the lotus pond to have a drink and a smoke together. I had something important to discuss with him, something that required his approval, so I wanted to get him in just the right mood for it. That meant getting him to sit down somewhere quiet and roll up one of his big holiday spliffs before bringing up my request. Whenever he smoked ganja, Lopper always listened with his heart, not just his head, and what I had in mind needed to go through the heart.

The idea had come to me the night before, while smoking opium with Moreau, and with each passing pipe it grew more important and urgent, until I became completely obsessed by it. Later, when I fell asleep, it manifested in a dream of such lucid clarity and emotional intensity that by morning I knew with absolute certainty that I had to do it. The only hitch was that I needed Lopper's permission.

He'd burned about halfway through his spliff, when his eyes began to glisten with that distant gaze that told me he'd shifted gear from hard-headed commando to soft-hearted chum. So I cut the small talk and came straight to the point. "I have a favor to ask, one that only you can grant."

"Name it, buddy," he said. "Today's the happiest New Year of my life and the dawn of a new dynasty here at Dragon Mountain. Your wish is my command."

"I'd like to have your permission to go out there and find my sons, make sure they're all right, and also to take my daughter Shana out of here, so she can get a proper education." I paused to let that sink in, then explained, "I've got two boys out there. Duncan, the older one, is twenty-eight this year, and last I heard he was living in Taiwan, studying Chinese. Frank is two years younger and was still in America when I left. It's been over ten years since I last saw either of them, and no doubt they think I'm dead by now. Since my wife died two years ago in San Francisco, they've got no one to look to for help. I'd like to go out and find them, let them know I'm still alive, do whatever I can to help them get set up. And I want to take Shana somewhere she can go to school. This is no place for her to grow up." I took a few drags off the spliff that Lopper passed me and handed it back to him. "So that's it. I rest my case."

Lopper sucked long and hard on the spliff, wreathing his head and shoulders in curling clouds of smoke. He blew a perfectly formed smoke ring and sent it swirling at me. "Granted!" he said. "I'll set it all up for you. I'll have Katz organize an escort party to take you down to the Thai border, and from there we'll arrange a ride for you all the way into Bangkok. How's that?"

"That's perfect. Thanks, Lopper, I really appreciate it. This means a lot to me."

"No sweat. Anything else?"

"Nope, that's all I ask."

"Then consider it done. Cheers!" We clinked glasses and bottomed up.

But there was more to it than that, and I wanted to clear it all with Lopper. "You know," I said, "I'll have to go straight to the American Embassy in Bangkok to arrange a passport and all that; otherwise I'll never get out of Thailand. When they find out who I am and where I've been, they'll want to debrief me in full detail. They're going to ask me a lot of questions about what I've seen and done here. You OK with that?"

"Hell, yes!" he yelped without a moment's hesitation. "Tell them whatever they want to know. And hey, don't forget to tell them how we rescued those POWs they left rotting in those camps in Laos, and that we're going back in there to get the rest of them out too. We should get a medal for that!" He clucked his tongue in mock indignation.

"I'll tell them that."

"Tell it like it is. Sing like a canary for them. It won't make a damn bit of difference. They've known about Ching Wei and his activities here for years, but they haven't done anything about it. That's because they're up to their assholes in the dope trade themselves, as you know better than anyone else. That's how Ching Wei nabbed you in the first place, remember? Our security here is guaranteed, because we produce the only international currency on earth—dope! For all I care, you can go back and write a book about what you've seen here. Who would ever believe it?" He burst out laughing and flipped the butt over the rail into the pond, then stood up and stretched. "Let's get back to the party. I keep forgetting I'm the host now."

There's not much left to tell. I decided to leave on the day of the Lantern Festival, the first full moon on the lunar calendar, exactly fifteen days after Chinese New Year. The Lantern Festival had always been my favorite Chinese holiday, so I thought it would make a memorable day to take my leave of Dragon Mountain.

The day after my talk with Lopper, I hiked up into the mountains to say goodbye to Ling Yun and thank him for all the things he'd done for me. *So you will soon be leaving Dragon Mountain,* he announced as he emerged from his cave to greet me. By then I was accustomed to his psychic prescience and simply nodded in affirmation. He often read my thoughts before I voiced them, and it saved us both a lot of breath.

"Where will you go?" he asked me.

"Back home to San Francisco—but with a stopover in Taipei first."

"Good, good!" Ling Yun's face crinkled into a big smile. *"There you will see your son, and there you will also find Master Lee.*

He will remember your meeting in the dream. Please carry to him my warmest regards—and also this." He handed me a ragged pouch stuffed with what appeared to be dried mushrooms. *"This is a very rare medicinal fungus that grows only in limestone caves in the mountains of southern Yunnan. Ching Wei obtained it for me at great expense. It restores and strengthens the internal organs, tones vital energy, and stimulates hormone production. For the promotion of longevity, there is nothing better on earth. Master Lee knows it well; it was his father's favorite tonic. He will be very happy to receive it, for it is not available outside China."*

We sat together all day long, drinking tea and talking. I filled him in on Lopper's coup and Ching Wei's dramatic suicide, but the details didn't seem to interest him at all, nor did he seem the least bit surprised to hear it. By the end of the day, I'd resolved to devote the rest of my life to cultivating the precious teachings and practices Ling Yun and Old Lee had given me. I knew that I'd been blessed to meet such great masters and that the things they'd taught me were the greatest treasures any man could hope for in this life.

As a parting gift, Ling Yun revealed to me the essential inner secrets of lung-gom—"wind leaping." I'd badgered him for years to teach me how to turn my legs into pogo sticks, but the most he'd ever done was to let me leap around together with him, using his energy field as a vehicle to carry mine. This time he showed me how to do it under my own power. He coached me on the little plateau in front of his cave until I got the hang of it, then we said farewell.

"We will meet again in this lifetime," he told me at the top of the trail. *"Until then, practice diligently!"* Then I hopped like a kangaroo all the way back down to Poong, hitting the outskirts of the village in fifteen minutes flat, a distance that usually took me two hours of hard hiking to cover.

When Loma heard that I was leaving soon, she didn't let another day go by without sex—urgent, sizzling hot sex—morning, afternoon, and night. She worked me like a pump, as though she were trying to fill up her tanks for a long drought, and several times she damn near persuaded me to stay. I wondered how

Moreau would handle her voracious appetite without me around to help feed it.

On the eve of my departure, Lopper threw a Lantern party at the palace for me, and I took the opportunity to say goodbye to all my old friends and colleagues there. Other than the formal affair on Chinese New Year day, this was the first real party Lopper hosted as the new lord of the domain, and it was as different from Ching Wei's style as night and day.

For one thing, everyone dressed comfortably in their own clothes rather than those long formal Chinese robes Ching Wei had always required us to wear, and the atmosphere was as casual as an American picnic. For another, the entertainment Lopper arranged actually entertained us and made us happy, rather than curdling our blood and chilling our hearts with fear and loathing, like Ching Wei's gruesome horror shows always did. There were some excellent performances of Chinese acrobatics and tribal song and dance, followed by a traditional lantern contest in which the children of the Chinese officers, the Lurps, and the village elders participated together to compete for prizes for creating the most beautiful lanterns. Shana was among them, proudly displaying the lantern Loma had helped her make for the occasion. It was a far cry from the blood and gore that marked Ching Wei's parties, and everyone clearly preferred Lopper's style of hospitality.

Lopper had eased into his new role as commander in chief at Dragon Mountain with instinctive finesse and shrewd insight, and everyone seemed genuinely happy to have him in charge. The transition had gone very smoothly, without a hitch, and business was better than ever. It would only be a matter of time before Dr. Hoffmann approached Lopper about his formula for China White and tried to interest him in the commercial prospects of producing it. If Lopper goes for it, there's no telling how much power and profit he'll acquire.

I was chosen to sit on the panel of judges for the children's lantern contest, and I noticed the Prince of Laos there among the rest of the kids, showing off an exquisite lantern of delicately knotted rattan and raw silk. The boy now lived in a luxurious villa of his own within the palace walls, attended everywhere by his entourage of young maids, and Lopper treated him like a brother, son, and fellow sovereign, all rolled into one. I tried one last time to find out more about him, but all Lopper said was, "Stick around and find out for yourself. We've got some grand plans. This is just the beginning." He smiled cryptically at me. "One of these days we're going to get us a real kingdom, with a real king." I'd never seen him so relaxed and completely at ease with himself. He was a natural-born leader, completely in his element now, and apparently well on his way to realizing his dreams.

"There will always be a place for you at our table," he said. "After you've done what you've got to do out there, if you ever feel like coming back, the door will always be open for you. Please remember that. You're part of the family now, and that will never change."

"Thanks. I'm really very happy to hear that. And who knows, I just might take you up on it some day."

The party broke up shortly after midnight, and I strolled slowly back home in the moonlight. It was hard to imagine that this would be the last time I took that familiar stroll from the palace to Moreau's place, and the last night I would spend at Dragon Mountain. Despite my initial enthusiasm for a reunion with my sons, I now found the thought of leaving Dragon Mountain oddly depressing. Where out there would I find another woman as luscious and lusty as Loma? Where out there would I find friends as loyal and true as Lopper and the Lurps? Where would I find a teacher like Ling Yun? Where would I go to smoke opium? The more I thought about it, the more certain I felt that some day I really might take up Lopper's invitation to return.

Moreau was still awake when I got home, waiting for me to come back and share a final farewell smoke with him. He was heating and spindling a fresh wad of opium over the lamp when I stepped into his den, and I could tell by the sweet, musky aroma that he was preparing the cream of the crop for me.

I lay down on my side and watched him work the opium in the glow of the lamplight. I'd always loved watching his hands prepare a pellet for smoking. With a silver spindle in each hand, he spun a gummy glob of black sap in the hot spot over the lamp, turning and twisting it, folding and molding it, like weaving an intricate knot with a pair of knitting needles. As it bubbled and swelled in the heat, the wad turned from black to brown, from brown to tan, and finally to that beautiful hue of burnished gold that only the purest, most perfectly refined opium produces when it's properly prepared for smoking.

"You're a real wizard, Moreau," I remarked as he rolled a cone on the surface of the bowl and inserted it into the hole for me to smoke. "I'm really going to miss you out there."

"Then stay!" he grumbled. "You will not be happy in that other world. I can guarantee you that." He passed the pipe over to me and guided the loaded bowl skillfully over the lamp as I smoked the golden nugget down to the last grain.

"You're probably right about that," I admitted. "But I won't rest easy again until I find my sons and make sure they're all right. After that, who knows, maybe I'll come back."

He brightened a bit at that. "You are always welcome here in my home, old friend. And Loma would be overjoyed to have you here again." Loma herself had made that abundantly clear to me over the past two weeks. We smoked and talked for a few hours, until we each drifted off into our own pipe dream, and I ended up sleeping there on the mat by the lamp all night.

The moment I emerged from the den early next morning, while Moreau continued to sleep like a stone, Loma grabbed me and took me into the bathhouse for one last bath and bonk. I wasn't sure which I'd miss the most: smoking opium with Moreau or making love with Loma. Together they provided a powerful incentive to come back some day.

Shortly after breakfast, One-Eye appeared at the house to fetch me and carry my pack down to the village, where Katz and the rest of my escort were waiting. One-Eye had wangled his way onto the escort party so that he could accompany me all the way down to the Thai border.

"*I will miss you,*" he spluttered, spraying a fine red mist into the air. Since I first set eyes on him standing in the cockpit of my plane nine years ago, I'd never once seen One-Eye without a cud of betel in his mouth. *"These years we have worked together here, they have been good. It is a pity that you must leave us."* When I mentioned I might come back to visit some day, he too brightened up, as though Dragon Mountain were a holiday resort where visitors were free to come and go as they please.

Lopper was waiting to see me off at the bridge near the edge of the village. He gave me the name of a shop stall in the night bazaar in Chiang Mai and told me that if I ever wanted to come back, all I had to do was go there and identify myself to the proprietor as "Captain Jack," then let him take my photo for confirmation and wait around a few weeks until the message reached Dragon Mountain and they arranged a rendezvous. He didn't tell me the name of the proprietor, only the name of the shop.

"Don't tell them the name of the shop when they debrief you," Lopper said. "It wouldn't do them any good anyway, but the old man who runs it is a friend of ours, and I don't want him getting hassled by those turds."

"I won't tell them." And I haven't.

Lopper gave me a big bear hug and wished me luck. As we headed down the trail, he hollered, "Don't forget: there'll always be a place for you at our table!"

I stopped in my tracks and turned around, scanning the green mountains that had been my home for nearly ten years. There stood Lopper at the top of the trail, waving goodbye, and once again I felt like the ambivalent pilgrim, reluctantly leaving his newfound friends at Shangri-la. I waved back and shouted, "I'll be back some day—you can count on it!"

**United States of America
Central Intelligence Agency
Bangkok**

To: Director/Covert, Langley, Virginia
Re: Operation Burma Road
Class: CONFIDENTIAL
Date: March 5, 1981

After completing his debriefing, we issued Captain Robertson a new passport and allowed him to travel onward to Taiwan to locate his son. After that he plans to return to the USA to find his other son. He refused to divulge the name of the shop in Chiang Mai that serves as a Thai liaison for that renegade LRRP unit in Burma. We suggest that you summon him down to Langley when he gets back and press him for that information.

We have not yet received any corroborating intelligence from other sources to confirm the death of the Chinese drug lord, Ching Wei, although we have no reason to doubt Robertson's account of that event.

Of particular concern is Robertson's testimony regarding Dr. Heinrich Hoffmann's purported discovery of the formula for China White. If true, this could spell big trouble. The stuff contains traces of what are known as "Bentley Compounds," opioid alkaloids that are at least a hundred times more potent and addictive than morphine, but we've never been able to figure out how the Chinese do it. They flooded Vietnam with China White during the war, and it totally decimated many of our troops there, but since the war ended we haven't seen much of the stuff around. Except for the war years in Vietnam, China has always kept a very tight lid on supplies of China White. If Hoffmann's formula is correct and it gets into the wrong hands, it could become a global disaster.

One last item of interest: we did some further investigation regarding that LRRP unit that went missing in Laos and ended up in Burma. Official army records state that they were sent into Laos to knock out a new missile pad the Soviets had installed there to protect the Ho Chi Minh Trail, but that turns out to be nothing more than a cover to conceal the real purpose of their mission, which had political rather than military objectives. Our own classified files from that period indicate that the mission was a harebrained scheme concocted by our station chief in Saigon, in conjunction with a reformist branch of the Lao royal family driven into exile in South Vietnam. The plan was to install an obscure young prince of royal blood on the Lao throne in the old royal capital up north in Luang Prabang, in a blitzkrieg coup secretly spearheaded by the LRRP patrol. At the time, the old regime in Laos was still an official U.S. ally, so our involvement in the coup had to remain completely covert. The idea was to quickly depose the corrupt old regime by enthroning a clean young prince as the new king of Laos, then letting the reformist faction return quickly to institute immediate reforms and win back the people's loyalty from the Pathet Lao, thereby forestalling the imminent Communist takeover of Laos. In retrospect, the whole thing sounds like a typical Laotian pipe dream, and we should have had the good sense not to get involved.

In any case, the mission was aborted when the LRRP patrol tangled with Ching Wei's squad and disappeared. The strange thing about it is that the young prince they were supposed to install on the throne in Laos was never seen again after that. Robertson's testimony clears up that mystery, but it still leaves the question: why did they take the kid with them to Burma? What on earth do those guys have in mind next?